CANDY APPLE KILLER

APPLE ORCHARD COZY MYSTERY BOOK 3

CHELSEA THOMAS

Big + LITTLE PRESS

To writers everywhere
The only way out is through.

1

MANHATTAN TURTLES

D riving through town with the windows down, I savored the warmth of the mid-September air.

Ahhhh, I sighed. *Nothing bad ever happens in summer.*

But, of course, that wasn't true. Trouble knew no seasons. And few people were more aware of that fact than I.

A year prior, I had been living what I'd considered a happy life with my fiancé, Mike, when he had dumped me. At the altar. On our wedding day. Then he had added insult to injury. He had stolen my interior design business and locked me out of the beautiful Manhattan apartment we had shared.

Homeless, jobless, and loveless, I had resigned myself to a life of Chinese takeout in a crummy Jersey City apartment. But my aunt, Miss May, had rescued me and recruited me to work on her apple orchard, which is why I had returned to my small home town of Pine Grove, New York.

At first, my transition from city life to country life had been jarring. I had felt out of place all the time. But then I'd adjusted. And I'd started to feel safe. And free. Like...*Nothing bad ever happens in Pine Grove.*

Three dead bodies later, I'd realized that I had been wrong. Bad stuff happened everywhere all the time, even in Pine Grove. But I'd also developed a knack for solving mysteries with Miss May. Thanks to me and my aunt, each of those murder cases had been solved and each killer had been caught.

Which brought me to that warm September morning, driving home with the windows down. As I cruised down Main Street, I realized it had been over six months since I'd found the last dead body in Pine Grove. The local denizens had been tense through much of that time. But as our unusually warm summer came to an end, the townspeople seemed relaxed and happy. And I felt that way too.

I had even chilled out enough to take my road test at the DMV a month prior, which I'd passed with flying colors. Yeah, I was a little old to be taking a driving test. But I hadn't needed a car in college or in New York City. I'd been license-free for almost ten years and I was more than ready to be back behind the wheel. Hence, my pleasant drive home from town in my new trusty steed — a rusty sky-blue pickup I had purchased from the local mechanic, Big Dan of Big Dan's Auto Repair.

I flicked the radio on as I drove and sang along with a country tune on the radio. The lyrics were about heartbreak, beer, and having the courage to forgive and forget. I didn't know that particular song word-for-word, but I did my best and mumbled over the parts I hadn't memorized.

Then my phone rang. I checked the caller ID, and my gut lurched into my chest.

It was my ex-fiancé, Mike.

I hadn't talked to Mike since he'd run out of the

church on our wedding day. And I had no desire to speak with him at that moment. Or ever again. So I ignored the call.

I'll forgive and forget eventually, I thought. *Just not today.*

Besides, I had work to do. Miss May and I were hosting the 20th annual "Candy Apple Hoedown" on the orchard that weekend, and I needed to hurry back to help set up.

Oh, and I didn't know it, but I was less than a week from discovering my next dead body.

Ugh.

When I pulled into the orchard, the trouble had already started. A woman paced back and forth in front of the bakeshop, crossed her arms, and then checked her watch. I had come to recognize these three actions — pacing, arm-crossing, and watch-checking — as the signs of an unhappy customer. So I took a deep breath and hopped out of the pickup with a smile.

"Hey there! How can I help you?"

As I approached, I got a better look at the woman. Late sixties. Designer jeans. Sweater tied around her neck. Costume jewelry that I could never afford. And a down-turned mouth that looked like it had been set in place some-time during the Reagan administration.

"I'll tell how you can help me," the woman said. "You can staff your establishment during business hours so that customers aren't forced to wait around in the hot sun. The only staff here is some sweaty farmhand, and he refused to let me into the bakeshop."

"Are you talking about KP?" I asked. "Big guy? Mustache?"

"That sounds like the culprit. Vile creature. Barked at me like a dog."

I laughed and waved the lady off. "That's just KP. He's from Kentucky. I'm sure he didn't mean any harm."

"Well, he harmed me," the woman said. "Why is this rotten farm so dreadfully understaffed?"

"Sorry about that," I said. "We're throwing a big party this weekend to announce the return of our famous candy apples. I was picking up supplies in town. How can I help you?" *Let's try this again.*

"You can introduce yourself, for one!"

"Where are my manners? Of course. My name is Chelsea Thomas. My aunt owns and runs this farm. I help her out."

The woman issued a forlorn sigh. "Chelsea. The name of my third favorite neighborhood in Manhattan. Alas, my life in the big, beautiful city has come to an end."

I perked up. "Oh. Are you from the city? I lived there for a while. Chelsea's beautiful."

"Don't you want to know my name?"

"I'm sorry. Yes." *Geez. This lady had a booby-trapped personality!* "What is your name?"

"Linda Turtle, of the Manhattan Turtles."

I coughed to cover a laugh. "Pleasure to meet you, Mrs. Turtle."

"My husband is around here somewhere. I sent him to find help." Linda pointed out into the orchard. "Ah yes. There he is now."

A sixty-something man trudged toward us from near the apple trees. He was balding. He wore bifocals down on his nose. And, like Linda, he had a sweater tied around his neck.

OK. I'll say it. He looked like a turtle.

Linda clapped in the man's direction. "Reginald! Hurry up. I found someone."

"Coming, dear." Reginald quickened his pace.

"This young woman is Chelsea. She claims she was not named after the neighborhood in Manhattan. I have, however, informed her that I love it and miss it and wish I were there."

"It's only an hour on the train, if you want to go into the city," I said.

"We can't afford the city," Linda sighed. "My brilliant husband Reginald — say hi Reginald."

"Hello," Reginald monotoned.

"Reginald squandered our retirement on a foolish European investment."

"I bought several thousand acres in the Netherlands that don't actually exist," Reginald said. "That's what I get for trusting my brother."

I stammered. "Oh. That's terrible. The land...isn't there?"

"That's what he said, Chelsea. Keep up." Linda shook her head. "Everyone is so slow upstate."

I may be slow, but at least I'm not a Turtle.

"My apologies," I said, doing my best to remain civil. "I'm sorry about your land."

"Yes," Reginald said. "As am I. As we all are in the family. My younger brother was never a good boy, yet I trusted his schemes. One after another. Until, well, we've told you of the land. It's not real."

Linda glared at Reginald. "We had planned to spend our retirement based in Manhattan, with frequent trips to Europe, or perhaps Bali or Dubai. Instead, all we can afford is this dumpy little town. So here we are. Pine Grove. Disgusting."

If I weren't on the job, I would have karate-kicked Linda Turtle in the face. But the Thomas Family Fruit and Fir Farm was famous for our friendly customer service, not our karate kicks, and I refused to let a couple of Turtles break me down.

"Well, Pine Grove is happy to have you," I said. "And if you give this dumpy little town a chance, I promise you'll grow to love it. We've been ranked a 'Top Small Town in America' for ten consecutive years."

"Yes. But not by any publications that matter," Linda said. "The Times, the Journal, etcetera."

I smiled, or at least I bared my teeth in the vague shape of a smile. "To each her own. How did you say I could help you today?"

"Right," Reginald said. "We were at the market this morning, where we overhead several people tittering in anticipation of your candy apples. I inquired about said apples, and an older woman directed us here. She was wearing a purple hat for which I did not care."

"Reginald, hush," Linda said. "You're telling it all wrong!"

Reginald hung his head. "I sensed your disapproval as I spoke. Please correct me, darling."

"The purple-hat woman did not direct us here," Linda said. "She informed us that the apples would not be available until this weekend. And that we should not come here until then."

"That's true," I said. "We don't sell any candy apples until the hoedown."

"Yes. The purple-hat woman regaled us with tales of the 'hoedown.' It sounded dreadful. Long lines. Local people. Horrid music." Linda wrinkled her nose. "Hence, we are here now, to purchase candy apples. Though descriptions of your hoedown struck terror into my heart, descriptions of your candy apples delighted me and caused me to salivate."

"We've both salivated over thoughts of the apples," Reginald said. "We eat sweets as a way to forget the pain of my foolish land investment—"

"Land investment implies there was land, Reginald. There was no land. Nor was there an investment. You gave your money away like a fool."

"Right," Reginald said. "We eat sweets to forget."

I tried to fight it, but my eyes widened, and my lips parted. *These people are too much.*

"You look shocked," Linda said. "This must be the first time you've met a couple for whom travel to Bali is routine."

Nope. This is the first time I've met aliens from Planet Snob.

That wasn't a hundred percent accurate. I had dealt with plenty of demanding clients from Planet Snob in Manhattan through my interior design business. But the Turtles took elitism to a whole new level. They were...remarkable specimens.

Linda waved a hand in front of my face. "Hello?"

"Sorry," I said. "I'm processing everything you've told me. Basically, you're here to buy candy apples before they're released."

"You're quicker than you look," Linda said. "That's what we're after."

I shrugged. "I'm sorry. The release is a big deal. We can't sell any candy apples until the hoedown."

"We'll pay three times as much," Reginald said.

"Reginald! Do not leap to squander more of our hard-earned money. This is what happened with the Netherlands! What's gotten into you? Do you need to see a brain doctor?"

Reginald cringed, like Linda had slapped him. "I'm sorry, Linda." He turned to me. "We can pay twice as much. Not a penny more."

"Um. I'm not sure about that," I said. "My aunt makes

the business decisions. I help with the baking, and I do the decorating."

"Get this 'aunt' of yours on the phone, then," Linda said. "We've already wasted ten minutes waiting for you to arrive and four more minutes talking to you. I refuse to waste more time standing on line at a ridiculous 'hoedown.'"

"Someone looking for me?" A voice rang out from behind us.

Linda, Reginald, and I turned in unison as Miss May marched out of the orchard, lugging a bushel of apples.

"Mabel Thomas," my aunt said. "Great to meet you. Most people call me Miss May."

Miss May put the apples down and shook the Turtles' hands. She listened as they retold their story about the woman in the purple hat. Once the Turtles finished talking, Miss May responded as I had.

"Sorry," she said. "If we sold candy apples to you before the hoedown, half the town would be up here trying to get an early bird special, and we're not ready for that."

"That is so stupid," Linda said.

Miss May smiled. "Not the first time I've heard that. I'm sorry I can't help. Hopefully we'll see you Saturday."

"Perhaps you don't understand," Linda said. "Economically speaking. We're offering you a two-times multiple on your candy apples. You can't afford to turn us away."

Miss May held up her hands. "I do understand, and I apologize for the inconvenience. If you'll excuse us, Chelsea and I need to get back to work. Feel free to stroll through the orchard. It's a beautiful day."

With that, Miss May unlocked the bake shop and went inside. I followed her, wiping my sweaty palms on my jeans.

Phewph. Crisis averted.

I glanced back at Linda and Reginald, who had returned

to bickering. Each time Linda yelled, Reginald's neck seemed to withdraw further into his shoulders. *Just like a turtle.*

It would only be a few days before one of them would be dead.

2

DECORATIONS AND DISASTERS

On the morning of the hoedown, I swung my sleep-deprived legs out of bed at the crack of dawn, and I didn't rest again until after I found the dead body.

But I'll get to that later.

Miss May and KP had been awake since before sunrise, decorating candy apples in the bakeshop. My assignment was to get the event barn set up before guests appeared for the hoedown at 5 PM. But I stopped into the bakeshop to say hi before I got started. OK, and for some baked goods. *A girl needs fuel!*

The place swirled with smells of cinnamon, caramel, and chocolate. And it looked like Santa's workshop, if Santa made candy apples instead of toys. Endless rows of finished apples lined the front and side counters. Coated in gooey caramel or toffee. Decorated with swirls of chocolate, sprinkles, and edible gold ribbons. There were blue sprinkle apples, and white chocolate apples, and apples crisscrossed with elegant butterscotch argyle. Miss May and KP worked at the back counter, dipping and decorating in focused silence.

My eyes lit up with wonder as I entered. "Miss May! These apples are incredible. Quelle artiste!"

Miss May kept her eyes trained on the apple she was decorating. "Not me, Chels. KP is the artiste."

KP waved her off. "Ah, ain't nothing." He paused and turned to me. "A few years in the city, you forget old KP is the man behind the curtain?"

My cheeks flushed blotchy red. Chagrin was not my best color. "I didn't forget!" *I forgot.* "How could I possibly? You are the Picasso of candy apples."

"You're not kidding." KP held up a candy apple with a sideways nose, twisted mouth, and uneven eyes. "Cubism at its finest."

I laughed. "That is very impressive."

KP shrugged. "I did a Van Gogh, too. But it didn't turn out so hot, so I ate it."

I smiled, but I felt guilty that I had given Miss May credit for KP's work. He had always loved doing the apples for the hoedown, and it was a tradition I had been part of for many years.

After my parents had died in a car accident, I had come to live with Miss May on the farm. I was only twelve years old, but Miss May — who viewed hard work as a panacea — introduced my nose to the grindstone right away. One of my favorite jobs had been helping KP prep the candy apples and I was disappointed that I had almost forgotten all about it.

As I watched Miss May and KP decorate on that foggy September Saturday, a pang of yearning noodled up my throat. I longed to be a little girl again, trotting along beside

KP and acting as his go-for. *Even when things stay the same*, I lamented, *they're never quite what they seem when you're a kid.*

If I could've time-traveled through my own life, there were a lot of moments I would have changed, big time. But there were also a lot of moments I would have liked to just visit for a while.

What a privilege it would be, I marveled, *to be a tourist in your own childhood.*

I snapped out of my nostalgia with a shiver and straightened my shoulders. Grown-up Chelsea had a job to do. That barn wasn't going to interior design itself. "Alright!" I said. "I should go. Don't get up to any trouble in here."

"We won't," KP said. "As long as those big city snobs don't come poking around again."

I guffawed. "How could I forget?! You met the Turtles yesterday! I would've paid good money to be a fly on the wall for that conversation."

KP dipped a Granny Smith in caramel. "Pay up, and I'll tell you all about it."

Miss May shook her head. "Normally turtles are such gentle creatures."

"Those two are a couple of snapping turtles. Only way to turn 'em nice is to cut off their heads." KP lowered his apple and turned to me. "So I'm out in the orchard yesterday. Minding my own business, working on a new irrigation ditch near the pumpkin patch like May had asked."

"Thanks for that, by the way," Miss May said.

"Of course," KP said. "Anyway, I'm running pipe out there by the pumpkins, and this fancy little couple charges up, walking like they're in the White House. Normally I would have pretended I don't speak-a-da-English, but I'm working on my customer service attitude. So I said 'hey.'"

"It'd be better to say 'Hi! How can I help you?'" Miss May said.

"Can I tell the story?" KP asked.

Miss May gestured for him to continue.

"So these two snapping Turtles charge up, and the woman demands I open the bakeshop. 'I can't open that shop,' I said. 'Can't you see I'm running pipe?' Then the woman mutters something about how I'm a sweaty farm-hand, and I gave her a suggestion about where she could shove it."

"KP!" Miss May said.

"I know," KP held up his hands in apology. "But she deserved it. I wasn't even sweating that much."

"So then what happened?" I asked.

"I told those Turtles to get off my back or I was going to bury them in the ditch I had just finished digging."

Miss May hung her head. "These are the kinds of things that hurt us in online reviews, KP."

"And I'm sorry for that, but I'm only human. Customer service is not my forte." KP rolled a caramel apple in crushed peanuts to underscore his point.

Miss May groaned. "Whatever. Those people would have left us a bad review no matter what."

"They were the absolute worst," I agreed.

"Amen to that," KP said. "I want them to go to their fake land in the Netherlands and never come back!"

I laughed. "They told you about that, too?"

"Talked my ear off," KP drizzled ganache in an elegant crosshatch over the crushed peanuts. "Told me about the Netherlands. Told me about their spoiled kid studying varmints in Africa or some such nonsense. Complained about Pine Grove the whole time! I said, 'If you don't like it here, I'll happily show you to the exit. Right there in that ditch. Just lay still while I pour on the dirt.'"

"Alright, KP," Miss May said. "You're over-drizzling."

"Am not!" KP turned away from Miss May and kept drizzling the ganache. It was definitely too much, but he wasn't about to stop.

"Well, it's getting late," I said. "I'm off to the event barn. Do you two need any help from me in here?"

"We're fine," Miss May said. "You've got a lot of work to do in there. Get moving already!"

"All right," I said. "KP, if the Turtles come back, I'll tell them you said hi."

KP scoffed. "Tell 'em I said 'die' instead."

Miss May hadn't said anything, but I could sense she was nervous about the hoedown that year. Business had been slower since the murder on the orchard the previous fall, so we needed the candy apple release to get the ball rolling for a busy season.

Yes, we had sold out of hoedown tickets months in advance, like always. But if guests didn't have a great time, they wouldn't come back to the orchard for apple-picking later. Nor would they visit the pumpkin patch around Halloween. Nor would they return to buy their Christmas trees that December.

Thus, I had resolved weeks prior to knock the town's collective socks off at the event, and I had worked all month to formulate and execute a sock-knocking design. The party was called a hoedown, so I'd chosen a country theme with a Chelsea twist.

In the center of the room, I had placed a 1950s-style dance floor. People would not dance if there was no dance floor, and I wanted people to dance.

I had also painted each dining table with vivid images of candy apples. And I'd strung market lights from the beams to give the event an air of sophistication.

Outside, I'd used hay bales to create a maze for the kids. I'd set up an elegant claw-foot bathtub as an apple-bobbing station. And I'd constructed a new makeshift fire pit beside the barn where people could sit and chat during the party. The circular pit was built of stones from the Pine Grove quarry, and I was proud of the intimate gathering space I had created.

That morning, I'd felt pretty bigheaded about all the work I'd done to prepare. But when I approached the event barn, my shoulders sagged, and my gait slowed. The barn looked lame, inside and out. I'd woken up thinking a few nips and tucks would complete the look I wanted, but it turned out that I'd have to perform something closer to reconstructive surgery to pull the thing together.

I took a few deep breaths and tried not to panic. This was not my first design nightmare, nor would it be my last. "You can do this," I said aloud. "You are a capable, resourceful woman."

Or at least that's what I keep telling myself.

I set to work. The first thing I noticed was that the dining tables were too far apart, as if to discourage socialization. I rearranged the tables and scooted them closer to the dancing area, which helped.

Next, I tackled the market lights, which were sparse and blah. My intention had been for the strands to suggest a minimalist aesthetic. But I had forgotten that the party was supposed to be a hoedown, not a New York City gala. There was nothing minimalist about a hoedown, so I broke out some of my more festive decorating tricks.

I kept the market lights up on the beams. But I also

added strands of red apple cut-outs. And brightly-colored streamers. And sparkly silver garlands, which I draped from beam to beam in generous lilts. Shiny was my go-to texture in dire design straits, and a reflective silver or gold accent never failed to brighten and liven a space.

Plus, every hoedown needs a little bling, am I right?

After three frantic and frazzled hours of re-decorating, I stood back to evaluate my progress. The barn had transformed from slapdash mediocrity into a bonafide party room. I smiled. *Mission accomplished.* Except the outside attractions were still missing pizazz.

In the last hour before the guests arrived, I dug up some old wooden planks from behind the event barn. I painted each plank with the name of an attraction, and I nailed the planks to a two-by-four that I shoved into the ground. The end result was rustic chic (even if all the hand-made signs weren't pointing in the exact right direction). I beamed at how I'd managed to tie everything together in such a short time.

Fixing a bad job is much more fun than doing a good job in the first place.

But no interior designer could overcome a dead body at her party. And that was a lesson I was about to learn for the second time.

3

OLD FRIENDS, NEW ENEMIES

Miss May smiled and waved as the first guest, a middle-aged woman, approached the hoedown.

"Noreen!" Miss May cooed. "So glad you made it."

"Made it!? I came back from India early to be here for this!"

Miss May and Noreen hugged. I did that thing where you awkwardly stand next to hugging people as you wait to be introduced. Miss May didn't let me suffer long.

"Noreen! This is my beautiful niece, Chelsea. I'm not sure if you've met."

"No, I don't think we have. It's a pleasure, Chelsea! You certainly are beautiful."

Noreen hugged me, which was unexpected. I stiffened but then reciprocated, relaxing into the haze of her warm and flowery perfume. It was a scent I could only identify as 'Woman of a Certain Age.' It reminded me of my mother.

When Noreen stepped back, I took a good look at her for the first time. She was plump, short, and red-faced, an apple of a woman. Her cropped gray hair framed her crinkled hazel eyes, and in spite of her crooked teeth, she had a dazzling smile. I assumed Noreen was one of Pine Grove's many residents descended from Irish stock. And I wondered if she was lucky, like a leprechaun.

"It's great to meet you, Noreen." I smiled back. "You have very striking eyes."

"Oh, well. I don't know about that. But they still see straight, so I can't knock them." Noreen turned to Miss May. "That reminds me! I got you something in India. Something you're going to love."

Miss May laughed. "You did not have to get me anything, Noreen."

"I wanted to. Besides, how else am I going to make sure you keep slipping me free pie?"

Noreen dug through her purse, then pulled out an ancient-looking book. Leather bound, with gold trim. I leaned forward.

"That's a cool book," I said.

"Cool indeed." Noreen handed the book to Miss May. "Go ahead. Give it a look."

Miss May opened the cover of the book. She smiled and shook her head, dumbfounded. "This is too much. You got this in India?"

What is it?! What's the book?

"Tiny book store. Next to a spice shop on a little street in New Delhi. I was shocked they had books in English. But they had tons. Saw this sitting there. Thought of you. Had to pick it up."

Miss May handed the book back. "Noreen. I can't."

Oh my goodness, somebody say the title!

Noreen pushed the book away. "Too bad! No returns, unless you want to fly to India and do it yourself."

Miss May opened the book again. "I didn't even see this. There's an inscription?"

Noreen grinned. "Just a little note."

Miss May read the note to herself and laughed. "You are too sweet."

I couldn't hold it in anymore, and I blurted out, "What book is it?"

Miss May grinned, "An Agatha Christie novel. *And Then There Were None.* My favorite."

"The original US edition," Noreen added.

"You know I love a good mystery," Miss May said. "This really means a lot to me. Thank you."

"Enough," Noreen said. "I just like to show my appreciation for the good people in my life."

"And your disdain for the bad ones?" Miss May asked with a smirk.

Noreen furrowed her brow. "I don't know what you mean..."

"Well, I was talking to Teeny, and she had been talking to Deb, and Deb said she saw Linda Turtle, that fancy newcomer, having a fit inside your dry-cleaning shop."

"Ohhhhh! Turtle, is that her name? I was too busy listening to her yell to make a proper introduction."

I chuckled. "Yeah, that was Linda Turtle. 'Of the Manhattan Turtles.'"

Noreen shook her head in amused disbelief. "And that meek little husband of hers. I almost felt sorry for him, poor guy. The only time Linda stopped yelling at me was to yell at him."

"Oh, so you met them both, then?" Miss May said.

"Well, 'meet' is a strong word. The husband was mostly sulking in the corner," Noreen said. "First, they parked that ridiculous luxury car in front of a hydrant. Then they paraded in right before my lunch break, lugging two enormous suitcases of clothes. Each!"

"That's a lot of dry-cleaning," I said. "Do they only own silk or something?"

Noreen turned her nose up and extended her pinky, doing her best Linda Turtle impression. "These suitcases contain our summer clothes. They must be dry-cleaned and preserved for next year before we place them in storage. We will be back in twenty-four hours to pick them up."

Miss May grunted. "They 'preserve' their summer clothes!? Like you would with a wedding dress? What did you tell them?"

"The truth," Noreen said. "There's no way I can do that in under twenty-four hours. And I've never heard of 'preserving' normal clothes before."

"KP got into it with them too," Miss May said. "Almost shoved them in a ditch."

"It's always interesting when city people move up," Noreen said. "Puts me in the mood for a candy apple!"

"Well," Miss May said. "I think you're in luck."

Linda and Reginald had made a lot of enemies in a little time. It seemed like everyone in town hated the Turtles.

Good thing turtles have a protective shell, I mused. *Otherwise, those two might get crushed.*

Fifteen minutes later, a big crowd had arrived, and the party was in full swing. A few bold twenty-somethings cut a rug on the dance floor. Older folks munched on candy apples at their tables. And Tom Gigley's cover band played "elevated classics" up on the band stand, each member wearing sunglasses and a Hawaiian shirt.

By day, Tom was the erudite town lawyer. So the sight of him rocking out behind the organ tickled me. And when he introduced the band as "The Giggles," I couldn't help but laugh out loud.

Miss May had asked Tom's band to adapt their usual set to an orchard setting, which Gigley and crew had obliged by replacing key words in their songs with the word apple.

"Lucy in the Sky with Diamonds" became "Lucy in the Sky with Apples."

"Bohemian Rhapsody" became "Bohemian Apple Tree."

Bing Crosby's "Pennies from Heaven" became "Apples from Heaven."

And my personal favorite... "Makin' Love in an Elevator" became "Makin' Applesauce in an Elevator."

Familiar faces dotted the crowd. Local architect Sudeer Patel indulged in a giant apple and tried not to drip caramel on his newborn baby. Brian from the Brown Cow Coffee Shop busted moves on the dance floor with his husband, Mr. Brian. And my cousin Maggie flirted with a cute guy by the apple-bobbing station.

People seemed to be having fun, and the whole room was abuzz with energy. And gossip. Everyone was talking about the infamous Turtles, and no one had anything nice to say.

According to Brian, Linda had yelled at him for making her coffee "taste of the bean." And Reginald had supposedly asked Mr. Brian for directions to the "closest world-class museum."

Even Mayor Linda Delgado, ever the polite politician, couldn't disguise her distaste for the Turtles. Apparently, Linda Turtle had called Town Hall fifty-one times to complain about the color of Pine Grove's fire hydrants. Seems they were "too red" for Mrs. Turtle's sensitive retinas. When Mayor Delgado had refused to change the hue of the hydrants, Linda Turtle accused the mayor of "besmirching the good name of Linda."

Still, most people were good-natured about the Turtles and optimistic that the snobby couple would spend whatever money they had left at local businesses. Plus, we all had a good time doing impressions of Linda and Reginald's hoity-toity accents.

But then the Turtles showed up at the barn. And the entire evening took a turn for the dead.

4

HOEDOWN HOMICIDE

When Linda and Reginald entered the barn, they looked around as if they had just landed in a bad neighborhood on Mars. Linda clutched her purse like someone might steal it. And Reginald wrapped a protective arm around her shoulders.

Miss May crossed the dance floor to welcome them. The Turtles may have been snappy, but they were still customers. And Miss May had the best customer service attitude in town.

I followed behind my aunt for moral support, and because I wanted to witness more Turtle madness. Miss May spread her arms wide in greeting.

"Linda, Reginald! Welcome to the hoedown! How are you this evening?"

Linda clutched her purse closer to her chest. "We're not well, if you must know. Reginald tweaked his elbow practicing his wretched golf putt this morning, and I've had to deal with his whining ever since. Isn't that right, Reginald?"

Reginald looked down. "That's right, darling. I have been a wretch."

Linda's eyebrows shot up. "See? He doesn't bother to deny it. He knows."

Miss May and I exchanged a look. The Turtles did not disappoint. "I'm sorry to hear about your elbow," I said.

Reginald rubbed his elbow and grimaced. "It's my own fault. I'm an aggressive putter."

"Aggressive and inaccurate, Reginald. Don't forget to mention what little talent you have on the green."

"I'm not good," Reginald said. "I've been beaten by a one-armed man."

It took all my willpower not to burst into laughter. Reginald's likeness to an actual turtle didn't help. "Is that true?"

Reginald nodded, but offered no further explanation. Linda clapped her hands together and turned to Miss May.

"Enough about this drooping excuse for a husband and his pitiful loss to a one-armed man. Tell me. Where can I buy candy and/or caramel apples? And what discount can you offer me as reparations for the way your farmhand treated me yesterday?"

Miss May blinked a few times, then regained her composure. "So sorry. We can't offer any discounts. But you're welcome to purchase as many apples as you like. KP is selling them, just over there."

Miss May pointed across the room. KP stood behind a folding table, selling his creations one at a time to a long line of waiting customers.

"KP runs this farm, all by himself," Miss May said. "And he actually decorates our famous candy apples. He's much more than a farmhand."

Linda craned her neck to get a look at the apples. "The candy apples do look quite nice. He's studied art? At a conservatory?"

"He has not," Miss May said. "Education is the enemy of creativity, don't you think?"

I snorted and tried to pass it off as a sneeze by loudly saying, "Achoo!" No one bought it, but I didn't care. Miss May was losing control of her customer service persona, and I loved it.

"I should hope not," Linda said. "I personally hold two graduate degrees in the arts. One in poetry. You may have noticed my eloquent speech. I thank my poetry degree for that. My other graduate degree is in oil painting. A skill for which I am ever grateful but never practice. Aren't I a wonderful painter, Reginald?"

Reginald nodded, but he still had his eyes on the candy apples. "Do you think it might be time to purchase and perhaps enjoy a caramel-coated apple, my dear? I'm fond of the peanut-crusted variety, and I think I spot one I'd like to claim."

"Yes, Reginald. We'll go now." Linda nodded at me, then at Miss May. "I would like to say this was a pleasure, yet I am in the basin of despair that is Pine Grove so I can not."

A few minutes later, Linda and Reginald were at the front of the line, face to face with KP.

I spied from across the room to make sure everything went OK. But the dance floor was crowded, so I could only glimpse KP and Linda once every few seconds.

Linda did not smile once as she spoke to KP. KP didn't smile either, but he gritted his teeth the whole time. At first, the transaction seemed to go smoothly. Linda pointed out her favorite apples and KP gathered them into a neat row near the cash register without giving her any trouble.

But Linda and Reginald did not stop at one or two candy apples. They kept asking for one more, and then one more, and then one more, and I could see KP's patience wearing thin.

Miss May sidled over to me. "How do you think that conversation's going?"

I did my best Linda Turtle. "And now I would like another apple. That one there. Good little farmhand. How dare you look me in the eye, you low-born trash!"

Miss May imitated KP's gruff baritone. "Hey lady! Keep it to yourself, or this'll be the last apple you ever eat!"

"Hush up and fetch me another," I said as Linda. "In Manhattan the apples are fresher and yield more juice!"

"The stores in Manhattan buy their apples from us, you crazy old bat!" Miss May growled as KP. She sounded so much like him I almost forgot we were guessing at the exchange.

Finally, Linda pointed at one last apple, and I swear I saw steam issuing from KP's ears. Linda pointed at the apple again, but instead of giving it to her, KP slipped out the back door of the barn. *Had Linda demanded the candy apple that broke the camel's back?*

I hurried after KP, but before I made it to the sales table, he had returned with a fresh box of candy apples and a smile on his face. He handed Linda an apple off the top of the box, then she paid him and sat down.

Weird.

Linda snapped in my direction before her butt even hit her chair. I hurried over, fingers crossed that I could remain civil.

"Can I help you with something?"

"You certainly can." Linda held up a candy apple by its stick and scowled. "How is one supposed to eat these?"

I furrowed my brow. *Was that a trick question?* "I'm not sure what you mean."

"I mean," Linda dropped the candy apple with a thud. "We don't have utensils. You know, the sharp pointy things with which one cuts and eats food? Are you familiar with these ancient tools of civilization, or shall I draw a picture? Oh wait! I doubt you know what pen and paper are. Would you like us to act them out? Reginald, stand up! I need you to pantomime for this young lady the essence of a pen."

I gaped. Linda's insults were so cutting, so original, I almost wanted to applaud her. I was tempted to retort, but I was no match for the woman before me. What would I say? *Uh, I know what a pen is, ma'am.* There was no point. Linda Turtle was a master of diminution.

"I'll get you a fork and knife," I said. "Did you want a pen and paper too?"

"Of course not! Shoo. Go away."

I nodded and rushed away. Miss May caught my eye and laughed as I grabbed silverware.

That would, however, be the one of the last laughs either of us would enjoy for the night.

The hoedown wrapped up around midnight. By all accounts, it was a huge success. Gigley and the Giggles had started to improvise apple tunes toward the end of the night, and they had returned for an encore with a stirring rendition of "Ain't No Apple High Enough."

Several formerly gung-ho twenty-somethings were asleep at their tables, drunk on too much hard cider. Plus, we had sold out of candy apples, and we'd received over two hundred pre-orders for Christmas trees.

The whole night had gone off without a hitch.

Miss May came up and hugged me as I scrubbed candy

apple coating off a table. "Great job tonight. You know how many people came up and told me how amazing the barn looked?"

"Oh, please. That was nothing. The apples were the real star." I paused for effect. "How many people though?"

Miss May laughed. "A lot."

"Well, it's easy to decorate a place that feels so authentic and warm. This farm is magic."

Miss May scoffed. "That's the hard cider talking."

"I haven't had any."

"In that case, go wake these other drunks," Miss May pointed at the sleeping twenty-somethings who dotted the barn. "They don't have to go home, but they can't stay here. But they can stay here if they're too drunk to drive. Just tell them to come in the farmhouse and crash on the couch."

"That!" I said to Miss May. "That's the magic. It's you."

Miss May nudged me away. "Will you go already? You're making me mushy."

I went from table to table, rousing the stragglers and offering them a place to stay. The first three were still tipsy, but the fourth was their designated driver — totally sober — so there was no need for accommodations.

Then I spotted one more sleeping guest in the far corner of the room. Her head was down, and she was surrounded by several half-eaten apples.

I approached and shook the woman's shoulders gently. "Hello? Wake up. Party's over."

The woman didn't stir.

"You can stay in the farmhouse if you don't have a ride. But Miss May doesn't want anyone sleeping in the barn."

No response. *Wow, this lady hit the cider hard. It's not even that alcoholic.*

One more shake. Still no response.

My feet tingled with a familiar sense of dread. *Uh-oh.*

"Please don't be dead," I said.

But the woman did not move.

"I don't think I can take another dead body."

I kneeled down and put my face on the table next to the woman's.

Her eyes were open and rolled back in her head.

I shrieked and stumbled back. I tripped over a chair and landed with a thump on my butt.

Linda Turtle's blank white eyes stared out at me. If she could have, I'm sure she would have ridiculed me for my clumsiness and lack of aplomb. But she couldn't say anything.

Because she was dead.

And Reginald was nowhere to be found.

5

KNOW WHEN TO HOLD 'EM

Not long after I'd found the deceased Turtle, Wayne arrived in his unmarked cruiser. I fixed my hair as soon as I saw him pull up. I scolded myself for being such a *girl*. But I couldn't help it. No matter the circumstances, my hands shot to my hair whenever Wayne was around.

"What happened here?" Wayne grumbled as he approached.

"I don't know. I thought she was drunk."

"Did you touch the body?"

"No! And I made sure no one else did either. This is not my first murder, you know."

Wayne sighed. "Yeah, I know."

Wayne looked around the room. KP and Miss May conversed along the far wall. Otherwise, the barn had been vacated. And the remnants of the party took on a spooky energy in light of Linda's death.

"I know this is your treasured family farm or whatever," Wayne said. "But it creeps me out."

"Good to know," I said. "Don't you have some investigating to do?"

"Yeah. I plan to start by questioning the person who found the body."

I scanned the room for Wayne's first interview culprit, then I realized...

"Oh! You mean me?!"

Wayne held up a calming hand. "Relax. I'm not accusing you. After three, uh, assists in murder cases, you get a pass on number four. Unless I find a good reason to suspect you."

"Oh wow, thanks," I deadpanned. "I'll get a punch card so you can keep track better."

I scowled at Wayne, annoyed that he was begrudging Miss May and me credit for helping in Pine Grove's last three murders. We had done a better job solving those mysteries than Wayne and the rest of the police force combined. I was about to say so, right to Wayne's smug, handsome face...but then he smiled at me, and my indignation melted like the Wicked Witch puddling on the floor.

"You look nice tonight," Wayne said. "Considering what you've been through."

A compliment. Oh no. I froze, unsure how to proceed. *Was I supposed to compliment him back?*

I hadn't been in this situation for a very long time. My ex-fiancé Mike's compliments tended to be backhanded. He'd say things like, "Your hair is better now that you don't have those weird bangs," or "That lipstick looks less gross than I thought it would." To which my usual response was, "Thanks, I think." So a regular, old-fashioned compliment from a regular old-fashioned man? Total curveball.

Speak, Chelsea! Speak!

"I haven't taken a shower in three days."

What!? Why did I say that? It was true but irrelevant. Just another entry in the long line of stupid-things-Chelsea-says-to-Wayne.

My confession stumped Wayne just as much as his compliment had stumped me. "OK. Well, I guess it's working for you."

"Yeah, I use dry shampoo," I mumbled.

I was about to karate kick myself in the face for piling stupid on stupid, but then I noticed that Wayne had stopped listening. Something across the barn had distracted him. "What's with that guy?"

I followed Wayne's gaze across the room. "Oh," I said with a dismissive wave, "that's KP. He's the resident jack-of-all-trades. Have you not met KP?"

KP cursed under his breath as he loudly collapsed the folding tables from the hoedown. Wayne narrowed his eyes as he watched KP work. "Do you know him well?"

"Yeah, he's basically like an uncle to me. He's worked on the farm my whole life. And you should see him with See-Saw!"

"See-Saw?"

"Yeah, our tiny horse. Have you not met See-Saw either? She and KP are basically best friends. It's adorable."

"Uh-huh. Right now I'd say your resident tiny horse-whisperer looks pretty upset."

"Oh sure, well, he hates folding the tables. Gets mad at them every time."

"So he has an anger problem."

I looked at Wayne like he had ice cream for brains. "That's not what I said. He just hates the tables."

"Does that sound normal? When you say it out loud?" Wayne asked.

"I guess not. But he's just...eccentric."

We watched as KP stacked the last folding table with a curse I couldn't repeat.

"KP decorates and sells the candy apples all by himself, you know. A lot of people are surprised to learn that."

Wayne pulled his detective notepad out of his back pocket without taking his eyes off of KP. He flipped the pad open and made a quick note. I tried to sneak a peek, but Wayne turned away as he scribbled.

"What are you writing?" I asked.

Wayne snapped the notepad shut. "Nothing. Would you be willing to introduce me to KP? I'd love to have a quick chat with him."

I scratched my nose. "I guess. What do you need to talk to him about?"

Wayne raised his eyebrows. "Official police business."

"KP is not a killer, if that's what you're thinking. His best friend is a tiny horse, remember?"

"People can be surprising."

"Not KP. He's very predictable." That wasn't entirely true, but Wayne was making me feel uneasy.

"Nevertheless. I'd like to ask him a few things about his whereabouts tonight."

"Then you can make your own introduction."

I brushed past Wayne and stomped out of the barn. *What nerve!*

Still, I couldn't help but glance over my shoulder at Wayne as I left.

He said I looked good tonight. I smiled to myself, then resumed my angry departure.

I exploded out of the barn and onto the orchard, expecting to find Miss May. Instead, I saw shampoo-spokes-woman-turned-cop Detective Sunshine Flanagan. Flanagan looked stunning, per usual, but I decided not to let it bother me. *So her uniform fits really well, so what? She probably gets it tailored.*

Then Flanagan reached back and yanked the scrunchy out of her hair, which sent her long red locks cascading down her back. I stopped in my tracks. *So shiny! Was this for real an actual woman's hair? She must shower all the time.*

I couldn't look away. I had never been hypnotized, but I imagined it would feel something like watching Sunshine Flanagan fix her ponytail.

Flanagan turned to talk to another officer, and I snapped out of my daze. *Oh right. I came out here to find Miss May.*

"Miss May," I called out. "Hello?"

A muffled voice called from somewhere to my left, "I'm in here!"

"In where?" I asked.

"In the maze!"

"Come out!"

"I can't find the exit! All I see is hay."

I hung my head. The maze had been intended for small children, but it looked like I had also created an aunt trap. "You need me to come find you?"

"Either that or arrange for supplies to be airdropped by the military."

I sighed. "OK," I said. "I'm coming in."

I entered the maze, and before I had taken two steps, I was already sweating up a category four storm. Not because I was claustrophobic in the traditional sense. I actually liked small nooks and comfortable, cozy spaces. But something about mazes freaked me the heck out. *They're designed to confuse people. To make you feel lost.* And I didn't need any help with that.

"Miss May," I called out. "Say something."

"Something."

"I'm not laughing," I said. "Seriously. I want to get out of here."

"Relax. It's not scary unless you think about how the walls of hay could collapse and crush you."

I wiped sweat from my forehead. And my knees. And my neck. *Uch. So sweaty.*

"I just found a dead body," I said. "Stop trying to scare me!"

"Sorry," Miss May said. "I was trying to lighten the mood."

"By stranding yourself in the maze?"

Miss May did not respond. I rounded a corner and ran smack into a dead end. I groaned. *Why had I designed a maze for this party?!*

"This is so annoying! Now I'm lost too!"

"I'm sorry," Miss May said. "Stay where you are. I'll climb the wall and jump to freedom."

"Oh OK. Let me know how that goes," I said. Silence from Miss May. "Let's do Marco Polo or something."

"Good idea," Miss May said. "You wanna be Marco or Polo?"

"Uh, I think they're the same guy."

"So?"

"I'll be Marco, I guess."

"Then I have to be Polo?"

I couldn't take any more banter, so I yelled as loud as I could, "MARCO!"

"Polo!" Miss May responded.

"MARCO!"

"You don't have to keep screaming Marco, Chels. I'll just say Polo, and you come find me."

With that, Miss May began to repeat the call of "Polo" at

the top of her lungs. The maze wasn't that big, so I knew she couldn't be far. But every time I rounded a corner, I felt like her voice grew softer instead of louder.

This is a literal nightmare. I have had this nightmare, and it did not go well.

I tried to steady myself with a deep breath and a meditative observation. "I am not lost. I am in a small maze for little kids. Nothing bad is going to happen."

Then, I rounded a corner and ran straight into a thick wall of hay. I lost my balance and fell backwards into another wall of hay. The force of my tumble knocked the top bale over the wall, and I heard a shriek from the other side.

"Miss May?"

A hand shot up from behind the collapsed wall. "Polo!"

I laughed and pulled the second bale of hay down so I could see to the other side. And there was Miss May, looking just as relieved as I was.

"We should have pushed the walls down sooner," I said. "I could have found you in thirty seconds!"

Miss May climbed over the last bale of hay. "That's a good lesson for next time. And for life, in general. Sometimes, it's easier to do the heavy lifting than to find a clever way out."

"Great teaching moment," I said. "Can we go now?"

Ten minutes later, I was cleaning up outside the barn when I heard yelling. I rushed inside to find KP and Wayne in a standoff. A matador and a bull, although I wasn't sure which was which.

"You're out of your mind!" KP shook his fist. "I didn't kill that crazy woman!"

"But you already admitted that you hated her," Wayne said.

KP laughed and shook his head. "Everyone hated her! Did you meet the lady?"

"You mean the victim?" Wayne said.

I didn't like the way Wayne was turning this around on KP, and I didn't like the way KP was shouting about hating the dead woman. I marched toward them. "Wayne! What do you think you're—?"

Wayne held up his hand to silence me. It worked. "This is official police business, ma'am. Please don't interfere."

Uh, ma'am?!

I resumed my march, in defiance of Wayne's hand. "You can't question KP like this. He doesn't even have a lawyer present."

"I don't need a lawyer! I didn't do anything."

Miss May's imposing voice echoed through the barn. "You always need a lawyer."

Sometimes, I forgot that my earthy, pie-making aunt had been a big-shot New York City prosecutor in a previous life. But she usually reminded me pretty quickly.

Miss May approached and stepped between KP and Wayne. "That's enough, Detective Hudson."

"Relax, May. I have this covered," KP said.

"No, you don't," Miss May said.

"I told this fool, I'm innocent. So what if I'm glad the lady croaked? Doesn't mean I'm guilty. I just have excellent taste in people. And that particular people deserved to die."

I took KP's arm and tried to lead him away from Wayne. "KP! Stop talking."

Wayne took KP's other arm. Like we were gripping two sides of a wishbone. "If the man wants to talk, let him talk."

Miss May grew two inches as she straightened her shoulders and got right in Wayne's face. "Let go of my client's arm, sir."

Wayne's nostrils flared. He glared at Miss May. She did not blink. She took another step toward him and crossed her arms. "Unless you have a warrant for this man's arrest, I need you to release him. Immediately."

Wayne let go of KP and help up a hand in apology. "OK. You know I respect you, May. Everyone needs to calm down."

Tension buzzed in the air like a hive of angry bees. I wondered which thing I was more allergic to: conflict or actual bees.

Flanagan entered the barn. "Hey Wayne, we're all ready to leave if you..." Flanagan trailed off when she saw the three-way standoff among Wayne, KP, and Miss May. "What's going on in here?"

Wayne swiveled toward Flanagan. "Nothing. I'm good to go." Wayne paused on his way out. "And KP? Don't leave town."

6

FIGHTING BACK

The next morning, we went to Grandma's to debrief Teeny on the Turtle fiasco. The restaurant was quiet, which was weird for a Sunday morning. Word about Linda's death had traveled across Pine Grove like a plague, so I assumed lots of people had stayed indoors, hoping to avoid murderers.

Petey, Teeny's teenage line cook, vacuumed the carpet with his headphones on. Other than him, there was only one person in the entire place.

The lone customer was someone I didn't recognize, which was also weird. The man was older, late 60s maybe, and he sat at a table by himself in the far corner. He had stringy hair tied back in a ponytail and wore a blazer with elbow-patches. The man poked at the eggs and bacon on his plate but didn't eat. His eyes drooped like a sad puppy from one of those depressing animal rescue commercials.

Granny, Teeny's mom and the owner of the restaurant, read a magazine from her usual stool behind the cash register. Teeny rushed over to greet us, darting past Granny so fast that the stool spun in a full circle. Granny seemed not to notice.

"Another dead body," Teeny said. "I can't believe it!"

Miss May shook her head. "No one can."

Teeny gestured at the man in the corner. "See that guy?" She leaned in and whispers. "That's Linda Turtle's brother. Akin, I guess. I told him breakfast was on the house. But he's like a vegetable. Morose. It's so sad."

I looked at the stranger. He didn't seem to have any of the pretension of his sister, and I wondered if they'd been close.

"You two want some coffee?" Teeny asked. "I just made a fresh pot"

"Sounds perfect," Miss May said. "Chels?"

"Sure. With ten creams, please," I said. I loved the idea of drinking fresh, hot coffee, but I couldn't stand the taste. "Actually, let me get a chocolate milk with a shot of espresso. I'll take it like medicine."

My phone buzzed in my pocket. I glanced at the caller ID and saw it was Mike. Again. I pressed decline and slipped the phone back into my jeans.

Moments later, Teeny brought us our drinks, then slid into the booth beside Miss May and we talked about Linda's death. Neither Miss May nor I mentioned the possibility that we might try to solve the case. But I secretly hoped Miss May was up for another investigation. All the murders that had occurred in town, horrible as they were, had given me confidence and purpose and strength. I wanted to have the chance to help bring another criminal to justice.

I was grateful when Teeny turned the conversation to our sleuthing. "So. You two are going to work this case, right? Find the killer? Put him, or her, behind bars for life?"

I was about to answer yes when Miss May shook her head no.

"I don't think so," Miss May said. "The police are sick of us. And they're right to resent our involvement."

"But they're so bad at their jobs," Teeny said. "Last week, they gave me a ticket for parking in my own driveway. $400!"

"That doesn't make sense," I said. "You shouldn't pay that."

"Technically, half my car was on the sidewalk," Teeny said. "But this is a small town! If you can't park on the sidewalk in Pine Grove, where can you park on the sidewalk?"

"Just pay the ticket, Teeny." Miss May poured herself more coffee. "And let this whole sleuthing conversation go. Chelsea and I need to focus on building more business at the orchard. We're not interested in solving any more mysteries."

Speak for yourself, I thought. Still, I stayed silent, not wanting to defy Miss May.

"Business is not going to pick up until this case is solved," Teeny said.

"That's why we're going to focus on starting a wholesale line of pies," Miss May said. "I want to get into grocery stores and gift shops throughout the state."

"You do?" I asked.

"Yep," Miss May said. "I woke up thinking about it this morning. And now that we're talking about it, I realize that it's a good idea."

"But what about the mystery?" I asked. "There's a killer on the loose."

"The police will handle police business. We'll handle orchard business. That's the way it should be."

"That's bull honky," Teeny said. "The people of Pine Grove need you to work this case!"

Miss May crossed her arms. "Sorry."

Teeny turned to me. "Chelsea. Convince her!"

I looked at Miss May. She glared back at me. I shrugged. "Sorry, Teeny. I don't think I can."

I looked away and took a depressed sip of chocolate milk. I wasn't ready to give up on solving mysteries, and I hated myself for lacking the courage to say so.

Once we finished our drinks, Miss May and I walked out to the car with Teeny. We were about to say goodbye when suddenly Petey burst out onto the parking lot and changed the course of the investigation forever.

"Miss May! Chelsea! Wait!"

We turned back. Petey dragged the vacuum cleaner behind him. He panted as he stopped running.

"Petey. What's wrong?" Miss May asked. "Everything OK?"

Petey shook his head and took another few seconds to catch his breath. Then he looked up.

"That guy. KP. He works at your orchard. Right?"

Miss May and I nodded.

Petey gulped.

"Yeah. Well. I've got bad news."

"Spit it out, Petey," Teeny said.

Petey gulped. "He's just been placed under arrest."

7

FREE KP

"Under arrest?" Miss May said. "For what? How do you know? Do you have a police scanner or something?"

"What's a police scanner?" Petey asked.

"Just tell the lady how you got your information," Teeny said. "No need to rub in how young you are. 'What's a police scanner?' Humph. Chelsea's young, too! See? Barely any wrinkles. A few crow's feet, that's it."

"Thanks, Teeny," I said. "I think."

"All the kids in town have been talking about it on Pictogram," Petey said. "My boy Lil George was at the police station when that giant detective guy pulled up with your friend. Lil George even snapped a pic."

Petey opened his phone and held it out for us to see. Sure enough, there was a photo of KP, scowling and hand-cuffed at the police station.

Teeny winced. "He does not look happy."

Miss May stayed focused on Petey. "Did your friend Little George–"

"Lil George," Petey corrected, emphasizing the lil.

"Right," Miss May said. "Did he find out, by any chance, why KP had been arrested?"

Petey shook his head. "Lil George just took the photo. He has troubles of his own to deal with."

"You need better friends, Petey," Teeny said. "Who is this George? What kind of trouble was he in?"

"Nah, you got it wrong. Lil George is good people. He was there to visit his parole officer."

"Hold on a second," Teeny said. "I have a whole new thing to be mad about. What are you doing on your phone at work?"

"I was researching a new recipe," Petey said. "That's the only way I'm going to be a real chef. You don't learn how to cook by vacuuming the floor."

"Now you want to be a chef?" Teeny said. "What happened to high school? I want you to go back to high school! There's nothing more valuable than a good education."

Miss May stepped between Petey and Teeny. "No one respects the value of a good education more than I do, Teeny. But one of my closest friends is currently in the slammer. Can we focus our energies on getting him out?"

"Good point," Teeny said. She turned to Petey. "Go finish vacuuming. Then fill out an application for your GED and put it on my desk."

We watched as Petey gathered the vacuum and trudged inside. Then I turned to Teeny and Miss May.

"So what are we going to do?" I asked.

"What do you think?" Miss May took the keys from my hand. "We're going to free KP."

Miss May, Teeny, and I were in such a panic en route to the jail that I imagined when we arrived the police department would be in a panic, too. Officers running every which way. Drug addicts cuffed and slumped against the wall. Punk teenagers getting roughed up by crooked cops. Detective Wayne Hudson overseeing the mayhem, drinking coffee and barking orders.

When we arrived, however, I remembered we were in Pine Grove, not New York City. The police department was nearly empty. No addicts or punks. And no Wayne, for better or worse.

There was only one police officer in the entire building, in fact. A skinny kid, maybe 22, sitting behind the reception desk. As soon as he noticed us, the officer jumped to his feet.

"Can I help you?" The young officer's voice squeaked when he spoke. *Did I say 22? Make that 14.*

Miss May crossed to the front desk in four powerful strides. Like Clark Kent donning his cape, Miss May had pulled back her hair in a slick knot and put on her most serious face. She was in full-on lawyer-mode and I liked it.

"Yes, you can help me," Miss May said. "You have arrested a man named KP Miller. This is a mistake. He needs to be remitted into my custody immediately."

The young officer grabbed a file off his desk. "It says here Mr. Miller is not to be released under any circumstances."

"I don't care what it says there," Ms. May said. "I say that—"

The phone rang, and the young officer answered, cutting Miss May off.

"Hello? No, ma'am. We have not located your missing feline yet, but the squad is out in full force conducting an investigation. I understand your concern. Yes. I understand that the feline is a biter. We'll be in touch."

"The squad is out investigating a missing cat?" Miss May asked. "Are you kidding me? You have a frail older man being held in this building without justifiable cause. If he is not released, I will seek retribution at the highest levels."

The young officer adjusted his collar and offered a weak smile. "I'm sorry...This is my first week. I can't release someone from custody without authorization."

Miss May slammed her fist on the desk. "I'll get the district attorney on the phone right now. Is that what you want? You want to make a fool of yourself in front of the D.A.?"

The kid stammered. "Uh...I'll tell you what...I'm not supposed to do this, but I can let you talk to him. If you want. Would that help? For like, five minutes?"

"Ten minutes," Miss May narrowed her eyes. "And I won't file a grievance with the district."

Miss May winked at me. She had never expected the officer to release KP. Getting to talk to KP in person was an excellent consolation prize.

"Are we going now, or do I need to use a secret password?" Miss May asked.

The young officer jumped out of his chair, fell back on his butt, then climbed up with a scared smile.

"Follow me!"

Once we were alone with KP, Miss May got straight to the point.

"Please tell me you did not kill that woman."

KP balked. "Come on, May! You know I couldn't hurt a fly."

"I have seen you kill many flies with great zeal," Miss May said.

"Fine," KP said. "You got me. I hate flies. But I did not lay a finger on that Turtle."

"Then why did they bring you in here, KP? Just because you were slamming tables around after the event?"

"I guess so." KP threw his hands up. "Chelsea's boyfriend has it out for me."

"He's not my boyfriend!" I said. "We're not even friends right now. I don't know what we are. It's complicated."

"Now's not the time to define the relationship, Chelsea." Miss May retrained her laser-focused gaze on KP. "The police didn't give you any inclination why they brought you in? They didn't provide reasonable cause?"

"Stupid Pine Grove PD," Teeny said. "Incompetent whack jobs if you ask me."

KP averted his eyes. "Actually. I guess, maybe, perhaps, they may have had reasonable cause."

"Uh-oh," Teeny said. "Did they catch you red-handed? Did you confess in a fit of rage? Is the Turtle woman your long-lost-lover from your secret life working as a Manhattan art dealer in the 80's?"

"Teeny!" Miss May glared. "Stop quoting episodes of the North Port diaries! This is serious."

"Sounds like a good show though," KP said.

Teeny smiled. "It's amazing."

"KP!" Miss May said. "Why did they bring you in here?"

"Oh. Uh... Well..." KP looked down.

"Just tell us, KP. That's the only way we can help."

KP nodded. Bit his lip. "I guess, uh... I did have what you might describe as a fit of rage when I was talking to that detective."

"OK..." Miss May narrowed her eyes.

"And I guess, uh, I got so mad that they were accusing me...that I told the cops they had permission to confiscate any and all of my property as evidence."

"KP." Miss May rubbed her temples.

"I know. I know! But I wanted them to leave me alone. And I had nothing to hide."

Teeny leaned forward. "So. What did they find?"

"They didn't find anything," KP said. "But they claim to have found arsenic in my candy apple kit. And, from what I overheard in the squad car, arsenic is the poison that was used to kill that snobby old Lizard."

"Turtle," I said. I had a bad habit of correcting people at inopportune moments.

"I know what her name is!" KP reddened. "Didn't you hear what I said? They've got me dead to rights!"

"A little arsenic isn't enough to convict you of murder. Is it?" I asked.

"I don't know," KP said. "It looks pretty bad."

"I don't understand," Teeny said. "Why did you have arsenic in your candy apple kit?"

"I didn't!" KP pounded the table. "I was framed."

I gasped. "No way."

"Bet your britches," KP said. "Someone killed the old reptile. Now they've got me hanging on the hook for it."

"Who would do that to you?" Miss May asked. "I know you have, er, some old grudges, but this—"

"I'm not sure it's even about me, May." KP leaned forward. "I think someone wanted her dead. And they used me as the patsy."

My mind flashed back to the hoedown. Linda had upset everyone in town in a matter of days. I could only imagine how many enemies she must have left behind in Manhattan. What if one of those people wanted her dead? Maybe the Turtles weren't just trying to get away from an empty bank account and some fake land in the Netherlands. Maybe they had a darker secret to hide.

A loud knock jolted me from my thoughts and back into

the present. Seconds later, Wayne barged into the room. And he did not look happy.

Teeny and I jumped to our feet when Wayne entered. KP scooted his chair back against the wall. Miss May didn't move a muscle.

"What is this?" Wayne said. "You are not allowed back here. None of you are."

Miss May gave Wayne a small smile. "Detective Hudson. So nice to see you here. I was beginning to think the Pine Grove Police Department had forced you into retirement for incompetence."

Wayne glared. "You need to get back into the lobby, now."

"Not going to happen, Wayne." Miss May pointed at Kenneth. "This man was coerced into providing evidence without understanding the significance of his actions. That is unjust and illegal in New York State. As his acting attorney, I demand his immediate release."

"The evidence we gathered was provided willingly," Wayne said. "And as far as I know, you're no longer a lawyer in the state of New York. So, like I said, get out."

Doubt flickered across Miss May's face. "I don't know where you get your information, but—"

"I looked you up," Wayne said. "You haven't been a member of the New York State bar for years."

"That's not true!" I said. "How can you call yourself a detective and be so bad at getting the truth?"

Miss May moved toward the exit. "Forget it, Chelsea. Let's get out of here."

KP looked up at Miss May. "May. Wait! What do I do now?"

"You sit tight," Miss May said. "We'll bail you out of here.

Right now. What do you want me to make for dinner tonight?"

"Steak sounds nice," KP said.

"No one is having any steak for dinner," Wayne said. "The judge denied bail. KP's in here until his trial. Six months to a year."

"That's crazy!" I took a step toward Wayne. "You can't do that! You have to set bail! It's the law."

"'This man poses an unacceptable risk,'" Wayne said. "Turns out your farmhand has an interesting history in the eyes of the law."

"That's not true," I said. "KP has worked at the farm my entire life. He's never gotten in any trouble at all."

"Sorry, Chelsea," Wayne shrugged. "Even uncles break the law."

As I left the police station, I had a conversation with myself that I'd had many times before. It went a little something like this...

"Don't cry, Chelsea."

But I always cry in these situations. KP is in jail!

"So what? You're a grown woman. Keep it together for everyone's sake."

OK. You're right, I know you're right. Deep breaths, deep breaths.

And then I cried.

I wasn't upset solely because of what had happened with Wayne and KP. I was also confused and overwhelmed by questions.

Why had KP been denied bail? What had he done to deserve that?

And why did Wayne think Miss May was no longer a

lawyer? She had told me a thousand times that she was in good standing with the New York State bar.

I wiped my tears to hide them from Miss May, but she caught me by the arm before we climbed in the car.

"Hey. Are you OK?"

I shrugged and sniffled.

"Nothing is as bad as it sounds," she said. "I promise."

"But it sounds really bad," I said. "What's going on with KP? He has a criminal record? Why didn't anybody ever tell me?"

"You were little," Miss May said. "It wasn't a big deal."

"Sounds like a big deal to me," Teeny said.

"It's just... It all started with some overdue books," Miss May said. "You know KP. He can be stubborn."

"So what happened?" I asked.

"According to KP, the library charged him overdue fees for two books he never even checked out. Way back in the nineties. He called them. Told them he wouldn't pay. But the librarians called him a thief. A liar. They insisted he pay the fees."

"Stupid librarians," I said. "Why are they all so mean?"

"Librarians are custodians of knowledge," Miss May said. "The severity of their attitudes reflects the importance of their calling."

"How much did he owe?" Teeny asked.

"Five dollars. Not even."

"Then what?" Teeny asked.

"Over time the five dollars became ten. Then twenty. Eventually he had a thousand dollars in overdue fees for books he said he never took out."

I hung my head. "Oh God. So what did he do?"

"Well," Miss May said. "The day he got the notice for the

thousand-dollar fine, he finally decided to return one of the books."

"But I thought he didn't have them!?" Teeny said.

Miss May threw up her hands. "Apparently he did have them. But he wanted the library to trust him. And he was offended that they accused him of not returning the books."

"But he didn't return the books!" I said.

"I know," Miss May said. "I know."

"Well, so what then?" Teeny asked. "He returned the books. How did he end up in jail?"

"He returned one of the books," Miss May said, "lodged in a heap of German Shepherd excrement."

I groaned. "KP."

"I would have done the exact same thing," Teeny said. "Sounds like those nasty librarians deserved it."

"But he had the books!" I said.

"It's the principle of the matter," Teeny said.

"But he had the books. What's the principle?"

"Do you two want to know what happened next or not?" Miss May asked.

"I assume that's when KP got arrested. For the book-poop," I said.

Miss May shook her head. "Nope. That time they just hit him with another fine. I paid it. The police weren't even involved."

"So then what?" I asked, dread rising in my stomach.

"Then he returned the second book," Miss May said. "On fire."

Teeny laughed so hard, she started to cry. My jaw dangled open. KP had always been impulsive, but I'd never seen him do anything like that.

"Yup," Miss May said. "And the librarian was married to the police chief. So he got arrested. And ever since then...KP has had a somewhat, uh, contentious relationship with the law. And he's bought all his books brand new."

"And that's why they won't set bail now?"

Miss May nodded. "Same police chief now as there was then."

I didn't know whether to laugh or cry. KP was a tough guy. Army vet. Grew up poor in Kentucky. Knew how to grab onto a grudge and hold it without letting go. But he was getting older, too. And jail is no place for anyone, especially the elderly.

I turned to Miss May. "So now are you willing to take this case? For KP?"

Miss May nodded.

"Let's find that killer."

8

TURTLE POWER

That night, Miss May made my favorite dinner, baked macaroni with homemade garlic bread. Although our family was mostly Irish, Miss May had learned the recipe decades earlier from her Italian grandmother. And the dish looked and tasted like it had been swiped off a Sicilian table and teleported to Pine Grove.

The San Marzano marinara was a deep, dark red. The local mozzarella was browned to perfection. And the layers of fresh pasta and milky ricotta were melt-in-your-mouth creamy.

We stress-ate our first serving in silence. Then I stood to get a second helping of garlic bread, and we began discussing the case.

"So," Miss May said. "Who do you think is our prime suspect?"

I shrugged. "Probably Reginald, right? I mean...he left Linda for dead."

"He literally left her dead," Miss May said. "Did you see him leave that night?"

"No. But he was definitely gone by the time I found her."

"I'm not sure he seems like a killer," Miss May said.

"But none of the murderers have," I said.

"That's a good point," Miss May said. "It's always a surprise, isn't it?"

I nodded and sat down with my second serving of bread. As I chewed, I remembered Wayne's claim that Miss May was no longer a lawyer, but I decided not to bring it up.

I figured Miss May would broach that subject in her own time. And Wayne was likely mistaken, anyway.

Although Wayne was the hunk to end all hunks, with his blue-green eyes, broad shoulders, and tree-trunk physique, he hadn't proven to be the most astute investigator. Anyone with even a quarter of a brain could tell that KP wasn't a murderer. *Although,* I remembered, *he did leave the candy apple table and come back with a "special" apple for Linda.* I shook off the worm of doubt that had just niggled its way into my thoughts and refocused on my annoyance at Detective Hudson.

The moment Wayne had arrested KP, he had gone from friend to enemy. And I wasn't sure he'd ever make it back.

The next day, we drove to Reginald's house. The place was in disrepair. The home was on Manor Drive, the fanciest street in all of Pine Grove, so I had expected the Turtle's to be dwelling in the typical opulent grandeur of the neighborhood. But the home was a modest old colonial. Paint peeled off the siding. Loose shingles clung to the roof. And weeds dominated the small yard.

The Turtles didn't strike me as the fixer-upper types, so I hesitated as I pulled up to the driveway. "Are you sure this is the right place?"

Miss May checked her notebook. "I'm sure. They bought

this house from Petunia. You know her. The woman who owns the flower shop? Barely a month ago."

"It's small," I said. "And kind of falling apart."

"There were only two Turtles," Miss May said. "I guess they didn't need much space."

"Still," I said. "This house looks condemned!"

"Chelsea. Be nice."

I threw up my hands. "Sorry. I'm just saying. How could this possibly have met Linda's standards?"

Miss May shrugged. "Seems like something we should ask Reginald about."

I climbed out of the pickup just as a buzzard whooshed down from the sky and landed between me and the front door.

Yikes. Not a good sign.

"Can we wait for the buzzard to fly away before we ring the bell?"

Miss May rolled her eyes. "Sure."

Miss May reached across my lap and honked the horn. The buzzard flapped its wings but didn't budge. Miss May honked again and the buzzard took off with an eerie quietude.

"Why'd you have to do that? I wanted to use that time to gather myself."

"If you're not gathered by now, it's not going to happen." Miss May pulled her hair back into a ponytail and trudged toward the front door.

I followed behind Miss May and tried to take a calming breath, but I noticed the buzzard circling above us and the air stalled in my windpipe.

Did that buzzard know something I didn't know?

Reginald came to the door before we rang the bell. I shot

a look at Miss May. *Next time, perhaps we could refrain from honking the horn just before we meet a suspect?*

Reginald was wearing plaid pants, along with a sweater-vest and a short-brimmed hat. A bag of golf clubs was slung over his shoulder.

He looked at us brightly. "Can I help you?"

Miss May pulled an apple pie from her purse and handed it to Reginald. "We're sorry to bother you. We're just here to drop off this pie. I know you must be going through a lot right now. Thought a little Dutch Apple might be a comfort."

I marveled as Reginald took the pie from Miss May. Somehow, I was still surprised whenever my aunt produced a pie from her bag. She had done it on every case we'd worked so far, but it always caught me off guard.

The pies always endeared me and Miss May to our suspects, and Reginald was no different. He held the pie to his nose and took a big smell.

"Cinnamon. Apple. Shortbread crust?"

Miss May nodded. "You have a good nose."

"I studied to become a sommelier. That's how I met Linda. So many years ago. I poured her an earthy red, which she spat all over the tablecloth and condemned for its 'essence of tire and filth.' I agreed with her assessment and asked her on a date."

Reginald looked down and picked at a fingernail. But when he looked up, he was grinning like he had just won the Powerball. "Boy oh boy, am I glad she's dead!"

Miss May laughed in shock. "I'm sorry. What?"

"If I had to spend one more fraction of a second with that woman, I would have ruptured. I would have turned inside out. Truly! My guts would have evacuated my body."

Miss May and I must have worn identical expressions of

shock, because Reginald straightened up and clicked his tongue at us.

"Oh, don't look so surprised. You saw the way she treated me. Like I was nothing but an earthworm. No! Lesser than an earthworm. What's lesser than an earthworm?"

"I don't know." I contemplated. "A beetle?"

Reginald scrunched up his face. "No. Beetles have legs. By virtue of that fact, they are superior to earthworms. By default. She treated me like a..."

"Slug?" I asked.

Reginald pumped his fist into the air. "Exactly. She treated me like a slug. And not a good slug, either."

I snuck a look over at Miss May. Her eyes were still wide, and she was unwontedly speechless. I tried to continue the conversation. "She treated you like a bad slug?"

"We covered that, Chelsea. I was a slug, yes. But I am a slug no longer! Today, I am, for the first time, not a slug. I am a man. And as such, I am going to work on my horrible putting game. My way of celebrating the death of my putrid wife, you see?"

I stammered. "Well...I would say I'm sorry for your loss but..."

"Not a loss, but a gain! Everyone who has ever met my wife should take today as a holiday. Do you know that every night she made me clean her feet? I did it once and from there, it blossomed into a hideous tradition. One of the innumerable hideous traditions of our insufferable marriage. For which I sacrificed my career as a sommelier."

"I don't understand," I said. "If all of that is true, why did you stay with her?"

"How could I not? For she was Linda Turtle. Of the Manhattan Turtles."

"Hold on. I thought your last name was Turtle." *Uh-oh...*

was this some sort of royal inter-marriage? Could the Turtles be kissing cousins?

"Sadly, you are mistaken. Linda forced her name upon me after our nuptials. I was but a lowly student when we met. Riches like hers I had never imagined. She dazzled me for the first year, maybe two. Lobster for breakfast. Lobster for lunch. Lobster for dinner and lobster for snack. We often enjoyed Broadway for our evening entertainment. She even paid for my sommelier training, at first. But once we wed, all my shiny playthings went away, as did the funding for my education as a somm. And from then on, I was a prisoner. Bound by golden handcuffs, as were so many Turtle men before me."

I didn't know what to say. But, as was my habit, I spoke anyway. "That's a lot of lobster."

Reginald gazed into the distance for five seconds, as if to say, "it certainly was," then he zipped back to reality. "Yes. Now, as I said, I'm off to the putting green."

Reginald brushed past me, down the front walk and toward his waiting sports car. But Miss May snapped out of her trance just as Mr. Turtle got to the driver's side door.

"Wait!" Miss May said.

Reginald turned back. "Well hello! The large elderly one speaks. I was beginning to think you had lost your voice like I lost my wife. I imagined, perhaps, that you had made a deal with the devil, as they say. Your voice in exchange for her life. That would have been sad, for you, but a necessary sacrifice for humanity on the whole."

Miss May balked. "Don't call me elderly, sir. You're older than I am!"

I swallowed a laugh. It was rare for Miss May to be so catty, but it looked good on her.

"And you should be ashamed," she said. "Talking about

your dead wife like that. Maybe she was right to treat you like a slug. Did you ever think of that?"

"I was not a slug! I had merely begun to think of myself in a slug-like way. But that was because I was a prisoner. And if you knew the bare facts, if you knew how she treated me... If you knew how she cheated? You would join me in a joyous jig upon her grave."

Miss May raised her eyebrows. "Linda cheated on you?"

"Twice a week. It was in her appointment book."

"She had adultery in her appointment book?" I asked.

"Yes. I wish I'd had the gall to confront her about her lover. I did follow her there once. To some ramshackle home deep in the Pine Grove forest. Alas, I did nothing to stop the affair. By that point, I was a shell of a man. No turtle pun intended. But, if you wish to give me credit for said pun, I will gladly accept. Can I go now? Why have you held me in such a way? At the precipice of my vehicle, at the precipice of the rest of my life."

Reginald spoke so quickly, and so much of it was nonsense, that his train of thought was tough to follow. But we got the gist. Linda had been cheating on him with some guy in the woods, and Reginald had never confronted her about it. What a sham of relationship the two Turtles had had.

Why is it that rich people always seem to have the most complicated relationships? Mo' money, mo' problems, I guess.

Miss May tried to bring the conversation back around to cordial. "Sorry for holding you up, uh, Reginald. I know you're not upset about Linda now. But her death might hit you hard later. You're new in town, so you may not know many people. If you need to see a familiar face, feel free to stop by the orchard. If we're not there, we're probably hanging out at Grandma's restaurant. Do you know it?"

"Yes, I have seen the restaurant. Cozy and quaint. Not for me. Besides, I'd rather not familiarize myself with anyone in this town. I plan to empty my social calendar entirely until my son Germany is back in the states."

"Jeremy?" I asked.

"Germany," Reginald said. "Germany Turtle. He's a good child. A scholar who has spent the better part of a year studying in Africa. Brilliant. He will prove more than company enough for me. Until then, I shall be a lone putter out on the greens. So please, no more invitations. Thank you for the pie though. Dutch Apple. How homely."

Reginald got in his car and pulled out, leaving us alone on his overgrown front lawn.

"Did he just insult my pie?" Miss May asked.

I shrugged. "I have no idea." I turned to Miss May. "We never asked why they bought this broken-down house."

"No need," Miss May said. "We're going to find Linda's lover."

9

CRYSTAL BALL

M iss May grabbed my keys and jumped behind the wheel of the pickup. I lagged a step behind.

"Where are we going? Shouldn't we sneak into Reginald's house and try to find that appointment book? If we want to find Linda's lover... That seems a good idea."

Miss May started the car. "Breaking and entering is far from a good idea. Especially now that we've made an enemy of the police."

"That's not my fault!"

Miss May peeled out of the driveway and the truck rumbled toward the main road. "No one said it was your fault, Chelpie. Calm down."

"If Wayne didn't want to make enemies, he shouldn't have treated KP like a murderer. Even if he did have evidence or something. He should've talked to us first."

"Why would he talk to one of us first? Do you think one of us has a special relationship with Wayne? I certainly don't."

I blushed and my voice rose two octaves. "That's not

what I'm saying, no. But we have worked with him on the past two big cases in town."

"And I'm not so sure he likes that," Miss May said.

"Whatever. Will you just tell me where were going?"

Miss May turned onto an old country road headed out of town. "There's only one place in Pine Grove that anyone would describe as a 'treehouse in the forest.' So that's where I'm driving. If you must know."

"Thank you." I looked over at Miss May. "And you think whoever lives there was, uh, the object of Linda's affection?"

Miss May took another side road. Deeper into the forest. "No," Miss May said. "I don't think she was cheating at all. The man who lives in the treehouse...is Salazar."

Miss May said Salazar with dramatic flair. The moniker was exotic, especially for Pine Grove. But I had never met anyone with that name, and I had no idea why it should mean something to me.

"Don't tell me you don't know who Salazar is?"

I shrugged. "Should I?"

"Salazar is Pine Grove's best, and only, psychic."

"Pine Grove has a psychic? How did I live my whole life not knowing that? Is he good? Have you had a session?"

Miss May shook her head. "Heck no. I hate psychics. They know more about me than I do."

"So you believe in them, then?" Sometimes my aunt surprised me.

"I didn't say I believe in psychics, Chelsea. However..."

I laughed. "...yes?"

"I find it's best to believe in everything, so long as it doesn't hurt you. It's good to keep your door open to the Universe. Otherwise, how will you know when the Universe shows up with a gift?"

I glanced at Miss May. She was a practical, hard-working

woman. Not prone to discussions of the Universe with a capital U. Yet somehow her philosophy on openness made sense to me.

That's what I love about Miss May, I thought. *Practical but imaginative, caring yet carefree, and perhaps a bit...spiritual.* I made a note to emulate those qualities in my own life.

"That's a good point," I said. "Who wants to miss out if the Universe shows up with a surprise present?"

Miss May turned down yet another deep, dark wooded road.

"So you don't think Salazar was Linda's...surprise present?" I asked.

Miss May wrinkled her nose. "Uh, well...Salazar is a good-looking man. But I suspect Linda only visited him for readings."

"She doesn't strike me as the typical customer of a psychic."

Miss May rattled to a stop adjacent to a rustic stone walkway which seemed to appear out of nowhere in the woods. The stones led down a hill, deeper into the trees. *Gulp.*

"Let's find out."

By the time I had gathered my purse and jumped out of the pickup, Miss May was already 10 feet down the path. I hurried to catch up, but the walkway consisted of uneven sheets of raw granite, and I nearly tripped several times. I recovered, took a step, and felt my foot plummet into a grassy hole. I lost my balance and toppled sideways.

Oomph! I landed on my left shoulder in a pile of leaves.

Miss May didn't even turn around. She called back, "Are you all right?"

"Fine," I grumped. But my sour mood didn't last long. As

soon as I took a good look around, my grouchiness turned to awe.

Maples, oaks, and evergreens towered above me. Translucent beams of sunlight filtered through the leaves. A brook gurgled over small, smooth rocks. And the stone path carved through the trees with such grace, my designer brain tingled with envy. Integrating design into natural landscapes was an *evergreen* (yeah, yeah, pun) challenge, and whoever had laid this granite had done a seamless job.

"Chelsea." Miss May's voice broke into my thoughts.

"Sorry. Yeah, I'm fine. I said I was fine."

Miss May looked around. "Beautiful up here, isn't it?"

"I had no idea this was here." *Funny how you can spend your whole life in a place and still not discover all its secrets.*

"Wait until you see the house." Miss May led the way down the path.

Once we crested the wooded hill, the house came into focus. The first thing I noticed were the varied rooftops. The main house had a steep stone roof, painted to look like a spotted mushroom. Off to the side were three domed turrets, each painted with bright stripes. Best of all? A heart-shaped weathervane completed the whimsical roofline.

We were there to visit a psychic, so I should have expected a quirky home. But that place looked like it belonged in a fairytale pop-up book, not in Pine Grove.

It was so weird that Salazar's house shared a ZIP code with the store where I bought my cleaning spray and applesauce. The home was not of this century. Or this world.

Miss May noticed my gaze. "Fun house, huh?"

"I can't tell if it's a fun house or a...funhouse. Is this guy roommates with a fancy hobbit?"

Miss May laughed, crossed to the door and knocked. We waited a few seconds, but no one answered. She knocked again. No answer. I noticed a blinking neon sign in the window. "OPEN. COME IN."

I nodded at the sign. "Look. Should we just go inside?"

Miss May tried the door handle, and it opened. She turned back to me. "Why not?"

10

PSYCHIC SURPRISE

The inside of the house was sleek and modern, a stark difference from the mossy, natural exterior. I wanted to hate it because Salazar the psychic already creeped me out, but I couldn't muster a single negative thought about the interior design.

The front room was slate gray, with a darker gray feature wall. A bright white fireplace and mantle popped against the deep gray. Empty, bright yellow frames decorated the walls, giving the whole place a satisfying, minimalist vibe. A yellow armchair and yellow flowers drew the eye around the room and made the whole space feel cohesive and inviting. *Dammit. Why did this have to be so good?*

Off to the side, a welcome table offered cucumber water, fresh fruit, and granola. *So many thoughtful touches! Who was this guy?!*

"It looks like the psychic business is going well," I said, gesturing to the high-end décor.

Miss May nodded. "Agreed. Sleek yet welcoming. No one ever accused Salazar of having bad taste."

"Who accused me of having bad taste?" A man's coy

tenor echoed in the sparse room. "I want names, addresses, and Social Security numbers. And make it quick!"

Salazar strode into the welcome area from an adjacent hallway. He was in his early forties, with bright white teeth, a well-groomed beard and deep brown eyes. Fathoms deep. His haircut was all sharp lines and straight angles, and it looked more expensive than my entire pajama wardrobe. He wore khaki capris and a white muscle shirt, an objectively hideous combo yet somehow it worked.

OK. I'll say it. Salazar was hot. Not my type. I will never love a man in three-quarter length pants. But I couldn't deny the magnetism of his presence.

Miss May smiled as Salazar drifted toward us. "Salazar! So good to see you."

"Better for you than it is for me," Salazar said. "I still want to know who accused me of having bad taste. There is no greater sin. Maybe a few. But those I've actually committed." Abruptly, Salazar shifted his bottomless gaze to me. "You must be Chelsea."

I side-eyed Salazar. *How does he know my name? Maybe he really is psychic.*

"That's right. I'm a psychic, so I know the names of every person on earth," Salazar said. "I wish! No. That psychic reading came free, courtesy of having lived in Pine Grove my entire life. So good to finally meet you in person. And I am terribly sorry about your failed marriage. I'm sure you didn't see it coming."

I touched my ring finger, where my engagement ring had once been. "Uh. Thank you. It's good to meet you too. I love your home."

"We both do," Miss May said. "We were praising your taste, not criticizing it."

Salazar let out an exaggerated sigh. "At last, I can

breathe easy! Thank you. This place is my living work of art." He clapped his hands together. "Now! How can I help you ladies? Are you both here for a reading, or is one of you in tow for moral support?"

Miss May swallowed. "Actually... Have you heard about how Chelsea and I have been solving murders?"

"Of course. Everyone has. Incredible."

"That's why we're here.... About Linda Turtle."

Salazar's smile disappeared. Replaced by a hardened look. "What about her? You know I can't divulge information about my sessions with Linda. Psychic-patient confidentiality."

"Are people who go to psychics really called patients?" *Oops. Did I say that out loud?*

Salazar shot me a sharp look. "That is the preferred term, yes."

Miss May held up her hands to calm the situation. "That's okay. We don't want any confidential information."

"I've already said too much."

"Then maybe you can say a bit more," Miss May said. "The woman is dead, after all. And if we don't find out who did it, the killer could strike again. Isn't there a clause in your oath for situations like this? Innocent people are in danger."

Salazar turned and looked at one of the empty frames, like he was viewing complex, masterful art rather than a blank space on the wall. "I suppose if I might be able to help... Perhaps I have a moral duty to do so."

Miss May pressed on. "Was your relationship with Linda more than professional?

Salazar scoffed. "Of course not. I would never use my powers to seduce. I've seen too many psychics go down that path. They lose everything."

"So she really was a 'patient?'" Miss May asked.

Salazar nodded. "She's been coming here for months. Long before she moved to the area."

"Really?" Miss May asked. "I'm sorry to sound so surprised. But she seemed like such a traditional woman."

"You never know who might believe." Salazar looked away from the empty frame. "I draw many of my clients from Manhattan and the other boroughs. City dwellers come to me, seeking solitude along with the truth. Also, I had a spread in an architectural magazine that helps business quite a bit."

"I saw that," Miss May said. "Congratulations."

"It was nothing. They spelled my name wrong. Still, it helped business."

"So when Linda came, did she say anything interesting? Anything worth noting?"

Salazar shook his head. "Not really. Certainly nothing that would lead to the arrest of her killer."

"You never know what information might help," Miss May said. "Could you perhaps share the general details that you learned from Linda?"

"I suppose I could share general details. But I want you to remember that during my sessions, I have a duty to help my patients find whatever information they need. Whatever is out there in the ether, I must harvest at their request. I am nothing but a medium. A tool that my clients use to dredge for the information they seek."

Clients? I thought they were patients.

"Of course," Miss May said.

"Linda came to me looking for advanced information on the Pine Grove real estate market," Salazar said. "She wanted to know what houses were going to be foreclosed upon, before the foreclosure proceedings began."

"She used you to find a deal on a house?" I asked. *Not the juicy details I had been expecting.*

"The whole process did make me feel used," Salazar said. "Though, as I said, I am nothing but a tool. The clay cannot judge the potter for sculpting an ugly pot."

"I guess not," Miss May said. "But that's all Linda wanted? Really?"

"I've told you everything I know." Salazar turned back to the wall and ran his finger along the edge of a yellow frame.

"What if...I bought a session?" Miss May asked. "Is it possible that, in the reading, new information might pop up?"

Salazar narrowed his eyes. "I never know what will happen in any given reading. Though I suppose it's possible that more information regarding Linda might surface."

"Then we'll take one reading, please."

"We will?" I blurted. Miss May shot me a silencing look. "I mean, we will!" For some reason, I sounded faintly Irish as I feigned enthusiasm.

"My sessions are not cheap," Salazar said.

"I know." Miss May smiled. "And I tip well."

Salazar crossed to a laptop and opened up a payment page. "And who will be my patient today? You or Chelsea?"

Moments later I followed Salazar into his "reading room," trying to hide my annoyance at Miss May for thrusting me into this bizarre process. Then Salazar killed the lights and instructed me to sit behind a hanging silk curtain.

I sat, as instructed. And that's when the chanting began. *Here's a summary*: Salazar repeated the word "MO" in a monotonous tone for five minutes, then he drew the curtain back and sat cross-legged opposite me.

"That was powerful," Salazar said. "And now we begin."

"Wait, that wasn't the beginning?" I said.

"No. The chanting was for me. To zone my energies so I could best serve you in our session."

Salazar reached out and grabbed my skull. It tickled. I laughed.

"Please. Keep your laughter to a minimum. It disrupts my vibrations."

I remembered Miss May's wisdom about being open to the Universe, and I put on a straight face. "Sorry."

"You apologize too much. Stop doing that."

Uhhh, what? Maybe Salazar was right, but I expected more fortune teller than life coach. Salazar continued before I had a chance to object.

"The vision is forming."

"OK..."

"Shh!" Salazar closed his eyes and moved his hands about in front of him as he spoke. "I see you. Standing in a kitchen. The walls are white, as is the floor, whiter than the whites of your eyes. The table is set for dinner, but the food isn't real. It's plastic. Everything is plastic. The walls, the floor, the furniture. Your whole life is plastic. Attractive upon first glance, yes. But you cannot eat plastic. You cannot sing a plastic song. You cannot live a plastic life."

Salazar's left shoulder shot back, and his head jerked to the opposite side. "The phone! The phone is ringing. But there you stand. Across the room. Like you too are made of plastic. A motionless doll. You must answer the phone. There is nothing to fear on the other end of the line. Everything you fear is plastic."

The logical part of me told me that Salazar was spewing nonsense. *Plastic? Dolls? Phones?* The dots didn't connect.

That was my brain. But my body disagreed. My chest

seemed to be stretching wide, pulling itself tight at the seams and opening up. Something in Salazar's gentle monotone felt otherworldly. The forest, the house, the waiting area...all of those places I'd passed through felt like other dimensions or other times. *Maybe I had traveled beyond the realm of the physical.*

"It's ringing," Salazar droned. "The phone is ringing. Why won't you answer?"

I thought of my parents first. After they'd died, I'd had recurring dreams that my mom or dad was calling me, but in every dream I either missed the calls or ignored them. Just like I'd ignored my grief, shoved it away to avoid dealing with an unthinkable loss.

My next thought was of Mike. He kept calling me, but I wouldn't answer. *Why?* I started to hear a faint ringing, which sent shivers shooting up and down my back. Was Salazar conjuring sounds of a phone from the netherworld?

Nope. My phone was ringing. Mike was literally calling me at that moment. My eyes shot open, and the strange surrealism of the reading vanished. *What just happened?*

I picked up my phone, double-checked the caller ID, and then I did what any normal, responsible adult would do.

I silenced the call.

11

FIFTY-FIVE AND OVER

As Miss May and I exited Salazar's fairy-tale house, my whole body felt wrong. My legs were jelly, struggling to carry me up the walkway. I felt like I'd taken my skin off and put it back on backwards. Miss May tried to make polite conversation, but I was in a stupor.

Had I just gotten a genuine psychic reading? Yes, the stuff about the ringing phone had been ambiguous. And it was probably coincidence that my own phone had happened to ring. But there was also all of that plastic talk.

As an interior designer, plastic was my enemy. Cheap, inauthentic, and ugly. But sometimes I'd used plastic in a pinch. That all seemed pretty literal.

But maybe Salazar's reading went deeper than that.

"You cannot eat plastic."

"You cannot live a plastic life."

"You cannot sing a plastic song."

What did he mean by that stuff? Was I living a plastic life because I was afraid to face reality? Why was I so afraid to talk to Mike?

Miss May honked the horn, and I snapped back to the present.

"Why are you honking?" I asked.

"To get your attention," Miss May said. "You've been off in Chelsea land for five minutes. We're already back in town. What happened in that reading?"

I shrugged. "Nothing." I didn't want to rehash the whole thing with Miss May. But she had psychic powers of her own.

"Salazar said something about Mike, didn't he?"

"Can we please talk about the case?"

"I've been waiting for you to ask," Miss May said. "Salazar dropped an enormous clue back there, but I don't even think you realized it."

"What clue?"

Miss May turned back onto the main road, exiting the forest. "Think about it."

All I could think about was plastic and ringing phones. "My brain isn't in the mood to think right now. Just tell me."

Miss May sighed. "Come on, Chelpie. What did Salazar say about Linda? About why she saw him?"

I picked at some peeling paint on the car door. "I don't know. The stuff about foreclosures? How is that a clue? It just makes me hate Linda even more. What a predator."

"Exactly! If Linda and Reginald were predatory about buying their house, that means someone was their prey."

My lips flipped into an impressed frown. "That's a good point. Didn't you say you knew the person who owned that house, though? The farmer's market lady or something?"

"The flower shop lady," Miss May said. "Petunia. Remember this morning, when we went to see Reginald, you were surprised that the house was in such disrepair? Now it all makes sense. Petunia didn't sell that house willingly. She would be too proud to admit it, but she must be broke."

"Do you think Petunia might want to kill the people who bought the house out from under her?"

Miss May slowed as a young mother pushed a stroller across the street. "Petunia is one tough gingersnap. I wouldn't put it past her."

The young mother waved to thank Miss May for waiting. Miss May waved back but didn't smile. My aunt was thinking serious thoughts. She needed all her face muscles for contemplation.

"What do we do now?" I asked. "Can we go talk to Petunia? Maybe Salazar was wrong. This could be a complete misunderstanding."

"We can't talk to Petunia until tomorrow," Miss May said. "She lives in Washington Village."

"The 55 and over community?"

Miss May nodded. "Their quiet hours start at 5 PM. Won't make it in time. But we can stop by first thing in the morning."

"Sounds good," I said. "Not good, but you know what I mean. If Petunia is the killer, we'll most likely catch her in the morning. Which is good."

"I get it, Chels."

"Good." I sat back and sighed. My thoughts drifted back to the reading, and I bolted upright in my seat. "Hang on a minute!"

"What?" Miss May asked.

"Salazar said the thing about the foreclosure before you suggested a reading. You already had the clue you wanted!"

Miss May kept her eyes on the road. "Oh. I didn't really think about that."

"Liar," I said. "You tricked me into a psychic reading!"

A hint of a smile tugged at the corners of Miss May's mouth. "Maybe," she said, "you have some sleuthing skills after all."

That night, I couldn't sleep. So I rolled out of bed at four-thirty in the morning and plodded over to the barn to visit our tiny horse, See-Saw. See-Saw measured 34 inches at the withers, which was on the small side even for an American Miniature. She had a reddish coat, somewhere between bay and sorrel, with a spray of white freckles on her haunches and a white diamond on her head. Her dark brown mane was cropped close, and it sprang up like a Mohawk along her neck.

Miss May had bought See-Saw when I was in high school and brought the little horse to the farm to make some extra money during off-season. I had spent hours grooming and feeding See-Saw when we'd first gotten her, but she had instantly preferred KP's company to anyone else's. He gave her treats and lovingly grumbled at her and took her for walks, and I was sure that she was missing him now.

"Hey, See-Saw," I said. I approached and pulled a carrot out of my pocket. See-Saw sniffed my hand and nibbled at the carrot, then let it drop to the ground.

"Not hungry?" I asked.

See-Saw chuffed and stomped her hoof, trampling the carrot.

"OK, sorry," I said. "So... you wanna talk about this murder case?"

See-Saw whinnied and flicked her tail. *Did I mention she was a good listener?* Not always the most open with her own feelings but more than willing to entertain my musings.

Over the course of the next hour I talked and talked, breaking occasionally for See-Saw to pee, poop, or chew on her own haunch. I told See-Saw about Linda and what had happened at Salazar's. I confessed that I wasn't sure why I was still avoiding Mike's phone calls, at which point See-Saw farted. I also tried to reassure her that Miss May and I were going to figure out this case and free KP. But See-Saw was a practical woman, and I knew that she knew that my promises were at least 20% horse manure.

So I admitted that I wasn't sure about anything. That I wanted to be strong, but sometimes I felt like a house with a vulnerable foundation. See-Saw nudged my face with her velvet snout, indicating her appreciation of my metaphor. From the way she nuzzled against me, I could tell that she, too, sometimes felt like a house with a vulnerable foundation. *We all do, sometimes.*

After about minute seventy-seven, I could tell See-Saw was getting restless. She flapped her lips and flicked her tail, so I tried to wrap things up. "In summary, Linda Turtle is dead," I said. "And so far, our only suspects are her husband and Petunia the flower shop lady. And I guess Salazar. He did have a creepy vibe, but also, I think he saw into my soul. So I don't know."

See-Saw didn't have much more insight into the investigation than I did. She was smart for a tiny horse, but not omniscient. If she had all the answers, she would've gotten KP out of jail post-haste.

I felt more relaxed after my chat with See-Saw, but I was also exhausted, and I needed coffee. So I gave See-Saw another hardy pat on the side and trudged away from the stables.

Not halfway back to the house, I ran into Miss May. *Hooray*. She was carrying 2 cups of coffee.

"I hope one of those cups is for me."

Miss May rubbed sleep out of her eyes. "Nope. One cup is for me, and the other cup is for See-Saw. She's been drinking a lot of coffee lately."

I laughed and snatched the cup of coffee away from Miss May.

"This better be mostly cream," I said, and sniffed the brew.

"Are you ready to hit the road?" Miss May asked.

"One second," I said. Then I took a sip of coffee and smiled. "All right. Now I'm ready."

Although it was barely 6 AM, the Washington Village resort-style 55 and older community, nestled on the outer edge of Pine Grove, was bustling. The only person who still seemed to be catching some shut-eye was the guard at the front gate. Miss May had to honk six times to wake the guy up, and he was so startled, he almost fell out of his chair. Then he handed us a heavy sign-in book. The thing weighed so much, I wondered how most of Washington Village's residents could lift it.

As soon as we pulled through the main gate, four elderly women strolled by, holding tennis rackets. Their legs were long and sinewy, evidence that tennis practice was likely a daily routine, and from the pep in their steps, it appeared the women had been awake for hours.

Next, we passed two elderly man working on sliding boards under their cars. One of the men slid out and sat up. He pulled off his shirt and wiped his face, and I swear he had a 12-pack. My eyes bulged. *How old is too old for a 29-year-old woman? Asking for a friend.*

Miss May parked next to the grease monkeys, and we climbed out. I nodded at the men. "Morning! How's it going?"

The shirtless guy squinted up at me. "I'm above-ground, and I know what year it is. That's good enough for me."

The guy was trying to be friendly, but I didn't know how to respond. *"Yup! I'm also happy I'm not dead or insane."* I didn't have the skill for that kind of repartee. So what I said instead was, "OK! Have a good one."

The grounds of Washington Village were laid out in a rectangle. Tennis courts, a pool, and a gazebo occupied the center of the rectangle, and apartment units and town-houses lined the edges of the complex.

Though I had never been to Washington Village before, and I had never met Petunia, I could pick out which apartment belonged to the florist from a mile away. Most of the units were gray and had simple patches of grass out front. But one home blossomed with a dozen neat rows of rose-bushes, tulips and daffodils.

I pointed out the house with the flowers out front. "Petunia's?"

Miss May shook her head, "No I think those are roses."

"Har-har," I said. "I meant…is that Petunia's house?"

"Oh, right. Yes. That's her place. Beautiful, isn't it? You can smell it from across the parking lot."

When we got to the door, Miss May rang the bell a few times, but Petunia didn't answer. I peeked through the little window beside the door. The apartment was cute. Over-stuffed floral couches, billowing floral curtains, and paintings of flowers on every wall. But all the lights were out, and no one stirred.

"Do you think maybe she's still asleep?" I asked. "It's early."

Miss May shook her head. "Not a chance. You saw the hustle and bustle out there. 6 AM is like noon to these people. Half of them are already on their way to early-bird lunch! And Petunia gets up earlier than anyone. She used to come to the bakeshop before we opened. Back when she lived close by."

I looked out over the lively pedestrian metropolis of the Washington Village luxury retirement community. "She could be anywhere."

Miss May shrugged. "Then we better start our search."

We scoured the compound, searching for Petunia. A dozen ladies practiced yoga in the gazebo, but Petunia was not among them. Another ten or so women power-walked along the sidewalks. Again, no Petunia. After we had questioned the tennis players and the amateur mechanics to no avail, I was ready to give up. But Miss May wagged her finger at me.

"We can't give up yet," Miss May said. "We haven't checked the clubhouse."

"Why didn't we check there first?" I asked.

Miss May opened her mouth to answer, but she clearly didn't have a good one. "It's early, Chels. I don't know."

As we approached the clubhouse, a din of conversation rose from inside. And rose, and rose, until it was a deafening roar of chatter. I hadn't been to a club that popular since my New York City days. *Ugh, fine, I had never been to a club that popular.*

Once inside, I understood the allure of the Washington

Village Clubhouse. As an interior designer, I often snubbed my nose at community spaces. They were practical venues, meant for hard use. But this place was exceptionally classy. High ceilings punctuated with vaulted skylights. Sturdy oak tables dotting the room. Winged leather chairs nestled into corners. And a king's spread on a buffet table along the back wall. I gravitated toward the buffet, but Miss May grabbed my arm.

"There." She pointed across the room.

"The food? It's the other way, actually."

"Nice try, Chels. I'm talking about Petunia. She's right over there."

I scanned the room, looking out over the sea of white hair, gray hair, and no hair. Then I realized... I had no idea what Petunia looked like.

"Which one is she?"

"Follow me." Miss May charged across the room.

As we got closer, I developed a pretty good hypothesis about Petunia's identity. A group of women played cards at a table along the far wall. One of the women at the table was dressed head-to-toe in floral attire. She had a frock of gray hair. Her sweater was covered in images of roses. Her leggings were covered in images of tulips. And she had a raspy, gruff voice that was a comical juxtaposition with her attire. The woman yelled at her table-mates impatiently and was clearly the leader of the card game.

Miss May walked straight towards the flower queen and tapped her on the shoulder. "Petunia! Just the woman I've been looking for."

Petunia looked up at Miss May with an impatient curl of the lip. The florist's voice was even gruffer up close, and she spoke with a thick Long Island accent. "May. What the heck do you want?" Petunia emphasized "you" like Miss May was an invasive species of weed. "I'm busy here. Too busy for you!"

Miss May balked at Petunia's rebuke. Usually Miss May was butter-smooth when it came to dealing with rudeness, but it was early in the morning and Petunia was being a...thorny flower. I took a step closer to get a look at whatever was busying Petunia. I glimpsed a few flashes of bling, and then I realized that Petunia's entire table was covered in coins, cash, jewelry, and poker chips.

From what I could tell, the women were in the middle of a high-stakes game of Texas Hold 'Em.

Petunia gestured at the table. "I'm in the middle of a game with these idiots."

"Ah," Miss May said. "Early for gambling, but I like it!"

"Early? This game's still going from last night, May! I wouldn't get up this early if all my grandchildren's lives depended on it!"

All right, I thought. *Maybe this lady could be the killer. Who casually references the death of their grandchildren like that?*

Miss May didn't let it faze her. "You've been playing since last night? All you girls must need a quick pee break. What do you think? Five minutes? I'd love to have a chat with Petunia."

Most of the ladies nodded. Many looked grateful for the interruption. But Petunia slapped the table, rattling the chips and jewels. "No! I'm in the middle of a lucky streak. What kind of hard drugs are you on, May?"

As Petunia spoke, another one of the women dealt a new hand. Petunia checked her cards and frowned. "On second thought," she said, "this hand is terrible. Reconvene in ten, ladies. If you're taking a number two, use the upstairs bathroom. And Ethel. You stay put and watch the table. Guard this booty with your life."

A skinny, thousand-year-old woman I presumed to be Ethel nodded at Petunia's directive and crossed her arms. Ethel seemed to be taking her job to heart, and I liked that. Then Petunia grabbed my bicep and pulled herself to her feet, using me as a prop. I almost toppled over. Petunia was strong.

"OK, May," Petunia grumbled. "You've got five minutes. What do you want?"

12

FLOWER POWER

From the outside, the floral prints in Petunia's apartment had seemed quaint and charming. From the inside, they were oppressive. As soon as we entered Petunia's home, the smell of flowers overwhelmed me. Roses overtook the kitchen table. Lilies obscured the back window. Tulips and lilacs of every color blocked the television.

What a weird woman, I thought. *Her face was so mean, yet her thumb was so green.*

"It's actually good you came," Petunia said, as she dug through a drawer. "I needed to take my meds over an hour ago. But I didn't want to show weakness at the table."

Petunia grabbed a tattered bag from the drawer and emptied it on the counter. At least a dozen pill bottles spilled out. She lined them up and began opening the bottles and popping pills while we talked.

"In that case, I'm also glad we came when we did," Miss May said. Her eyes widened as Petunia downed a millionth pill. "Have you been feeling OK?"

For real. All those pills, you hope someone isn't sick.

"I'm fine," Petunia said. "The doctor says it's good to take preemptive medicines."

I squinted at the bottles of medication. Those looked like prescriptions, not daily vitamins. But I did not want to argue with Petunia. Besides, we were there on an official, unofficial investigation about a murder. Not about Petunia's potential abuse of pills.

Petunia downed three enormous tablets at the same time, along with a big sip of black coffee which must've been sitting on the counter since the day before. *Gross.* I grimaced and averted my eyes. Everywhere I looked, flowers seemed to be actively encroaching on the space. *I think I've literally had this nightmare.*

I tried to use my interior design brain to see past the flowers. *What would I do if I could redecorate?* I asked myself. *How are the bones of this apartment?* I noticed that Petunia's unit had a handful of classy antique finishes. Her light fixtures were 19th century brushed copper. And her door-knobs were also antique. Pretty nice for a 55 and up joint. Somehow, I doubted that every apartment was so well-appointed.

"Did you see that girl, Ethel?" Petunia asked. "Do you think I can trust her? This is the first time I put her on money duty during a bathroom break. Sometimes the girls skim off the top. I hope I didn't make a mistake with Ethel."

Ethel was so old that I doubted she could be trusted to remember her own name. But I didn't voice my concerns. I was pretty afraid of rankling Petunia.

Miss May chuckled. "I'm sure Ethel can be trusted in a little card game."

"That's not a little card game, May. There was at least $10,000 in jewelry on that last hand. We've all accumulated so many nice things over the years, these games are high-stakes, even by Vegas standards. What else are we going to do with our stuff? Leave it to our grandkids? Why? So they can go to college? I didn't go to college, and I had a great life."

At that, Petunia burst into hoarse laughter.

I take it she does not have a great relationship with her grandchildren, I thought.

"Ethel seemed trustworthy to me," I said, trying to scoot the conversation back toward the murdered Turtle.

"Good," Petunia turned to Miss May. "Now get to it. What do you want?" *Here we go.*

Miss May calibrated to her gentlest voice. "Actually, I wanted to ask you about your, uh, old house."

"What about it?"

"Well..." Miss May fingered a wilting tulip. "There's no easy way to put this... "

"Spit it out!" Petunia barked.

"I know you said you sold the place, but—"

"I did sell it. I got good money for it. I would've kept it for another hundred years, but the place is too big for one old lady. The stairs didn't bother me, for the record. I'm great with stairs. I do 10 flights a day, with a cigarette in my mouth."

"Really?" *Dammit, why did I say that? And why did I say it like that?*

"You don't believe me? I'll light one up and give you twenty right now."

As curious as I was to see that spectacle, I shook my head and gazed at the floor.

Petunia grunted. "That's what I thought. What do you want with the house anyway? The place is off the market."

Miss May proceeded with caution. "That's the thing.

Was it ever on the market? I don't want to offend you...but is it possible, perhaps, that the home was foreclosed upon?"

Petunia slammed a pill bottle down on the counter. The lid wasn't on tight, and pills erupted from the bottle and scattered across the Formica. Petunia didn't seem to notice. She glared at Miss May. "Unbelievable."

"I know, Petunia. And I'm sorry that I have to ask."

"You don't have to do anything! You're here because you want to be." Petunia thrust one pill bottle after another back into her bag, shaking her head. "And now I want you to leave."

Miss May wasn't giving up so easily. "So the house wasn't foreclosed upon?"

"No," Petunia shouted. "I'm not some homeless bum. I chose to sell that house."

"OK," Miss May said. "I'm not trying to insult you, Petunia. You know I have nothing but respect for you and your flowers. It's just...well, the woman who bought your former abode is dead now."

"And good riddance." Petunia poured herself another cup of black coffee. "Linda Turtle was a scourge on Pine Grove. You met her, right?"

Miss May nodded. "She was a difficult personality. But sometimes difficult people are sweet inside. Don't you think?"

Petunia scoffed. "I think that Turtle was rotten to the shell." *That didn't make sense, I thought. But I held my tongue.*

Petunia's hand trembled slightly as she sipped her day-old brew. "I could have paid off that house, if they had given me more time. You saw that spread on the card table. I have funds. Don't think of me like some homeless bum."

What did this lady have against the homeless?

"No one thinks of you that way," Miss May said. "Foreclosure happens to tons of people."

"But I'm not like those people. Those people are bums. Homeless bums! I'm telling you, I could have paid. I just, I ignored the notices until it was too late. I hate mail. I never open it. When they showed up to take my house, I didn't have the liquidity to pay them right away. So they sold it out from under me. Taxes! The greatest scam ever perpetrated on the American people. Isn't this why we threw the tea overboard?"

"I think that had more to do with taxation without representation." *Welp, so much for holding my tongue.* I wanted to stop talking but I couldn't. "The colonists didn't object to the taxes entirely," I said. "They just wanted to have a say in who taxed them."

Miss May held up a hand to stop me. "OK, Chelsea." She turned back to Petunia. "Sounds like Linda and Reginald took advantage of an unfortunate situation."

"That's a kind way to say it." Petunia leaned on the counter. "That house had been in my family for 96 years. Almost a century. We moved there when I was only two years old."

"You're 98?!" I covered my mouth. *Stupid tongue, just couldn't sit still.* "Sorry. You look amazing for 98. I thought you were maybe 78, at most."

Petunia furrowed her brow. "May. You bring this girl out in public? Does she have irritable bowel syndrome of the mouth? Does she have a leaky brain? Because I have medicine for that stuff."

Miss May laughed. Petunia allowed a grudging chuckle, but it quickly morphed into a hacking cough. Still, my stupidity had smashed the tension to pieces. I let out a sigh I didn't know I was holding.

"A brain pill sounds great," I joked.

Petunia grabbed her bag full of pills, not joking at all. "What flavor do you like? Orange, strawberry, or whiskey sour? I'm not kidding."

We laughed again. Petunia smacked Miss May on the back.

"It's good to see you, May. Even if you are here to back-handedly accuse me of murder. But I blame the government for losing my house more than I blame that horrible dead lady and her slimy husband. So go find someone else to suspect."

"Petunia...I'm not...we don't..." Miss May stammered.

"Ninety-eight years, I know when I'm suspected of something, May. Hey, I get it. No hard feelings. Whatever."

Ethel, the old woman who Petunia had left in charge of the money, poked her head into the apartment. "Petunia? Ladies are antsy. They want to start."

Petunia turned on Ethel. "Ethel! If you're here, who's watching the pot?" Ethel scratched her head. Petunia crossed over to the door and held it open for us to leave. "I knew I couldn't trust her," Petunia muttered. "Alright, May. I've got bigger fish to fillet. Out!"

"Fish to fry," I muttered. Thank goodness Petunia didn't hear me, or that would've probably gone down in history as the day I got punched by an old lady.

Miss May and I exited, with Petunia and Ethel right behind us. We watched as Petunia scolded Ethel all the way back to the clubhouse.

"That lady is something," I said.

"Yeah, Petunia is a character." Miss May smiled as we watched her go, but the smile faded. "Do you think she could have killed Linda?"

"I hope not," I said. "She grew on me after a while."

"She does that," Miss May said. "But I still think she's hiding something."

13

HAWAIIAN HORROR

Miss May wanted to check in with KP and update him on the case, so our next stop after Petunia's was the police station.

As we approached, I worked my anger at Wayne into a rich and foamy lather and vowed to give him a piece of my mind as soon as we entered the station. But as it turned out, it was all for naught because the place was empty.

In fact, just like our prior visit, the only person in the entire department was the young officer standing at the front desk. He was on the phone as we entered, so we waited patiently for him to finish.

The officer gulped as he listened to the voice on the other end of the line. Occasionally, the officer said something like "Of course," or "We're taking this matter seriously." But for the most part, he just stood there, sweating. I almost started to sympathy-sweat, wondering what serious thing could demand such urgency. Then the officer said, "Missing cats and dogs are a top priority for this department," and I laughed.

Hearing the echo of my laughter, the officer finally realized he had company. He hung up the phone and cleared his throat. He did his best impression of an authoritative voice, but the kid was so young and squeaky, he looked and sounded like he was dressed up as a cop to go trick-or-treating. "Hello. What can I help you with? Is there crime you would like to support? I mean report!"

Miss May chuckled. "Where are all the other officers? Out rescuing cats from trees?"

The officer put on his best serious face. "If by 'rescuing cats,' you mean 'solving murders,' then yes."

"This isn't a competition, you know. We all want the murderer behind bars. So I hope you're right." Miss May's tone surprised the officer.

"Oh. Yeah. Well, that's what they're doing, I think. I mean, they are also helping with some lost pets. But generally, I think they're somewhere in the process of murder-solving, so..." The officer interrupted his own rambling. "Are you here to report a crime or not?"

"Not quite," Miss May said. "We're here to talk to your prisoner. KP? We were in here the other day. Have you forgotten us already?"

The officer stood and puffed out his chest. "I do recall your previous appearance. Unfortunately, you will not be permitted to visit with Mr. Miller at this time. Visitors are not welcome at this department unless it is during official visiting hours." The way the officer spoke, it sounded like he was reciting something Detective Wayne Hudson had forced him to memorize.

Miss May leaned forward. "I'm sorry, what did you say your name was?"

The officer cleared his throat, once again. "My name is Hercules."

I giggled. *Not exactly apt.*

"Hercules. What a wonderful name. Well, I'm sorry to tell you, Herc, but visiting hours are right now."

Hercules narrowed his eyes. "They are?"

Miss May pointed at a sign behind the officer. Visiting hours: 9 AM through 1 PM. Daily.

Hercules took on inordinate amount of time to read the sign, then turned back to us. "Oh."

When we sat down with KP in the visiting room, he looked exhausted. Big bags hung under his eyes. Grease matted his hair to his head. And somehow, he had gained significant weight in only three days. Not good.

He smiled when he saw us, and his grin erased the wear on his face. He seemed happy to hear how hard we had been working the case. But as Miss May dove into the details, KP seemed to be losing hours of sleep right in front of us.

Each time Miss May mentioned a new suspect, KP insisted that person was guilty. He was so desperate to get out of jail, he barely let Miss May speak before pounding his fist after every name.

"The husband did it! I knew it!" "The flower lady! I knew she was a maniac!" "Psychics can never be trusted. That's a fact!"

KP also suggested that the mayor could have killed Mrs. Turtle, for a particularly outlandish reason. "This town wasn't big enough for two Lindas! Linda Delgado killed Linda Turtle to even the field."

When Miss May dismissed the two-Linda theory, KP said he suspected that Linda's brother Dennis could have done it. Then he went totally off the rails and asked Miss May if she thought it were possible that aliens could have committed the crime.

At first, Miss May was patient with KP. But at the mention of aliens she put her foot down.

"KP. This crime was not committed by extra-terrestrials. You need to get a grip."

"I don't care who did it, I just want to get out of here!"

Miss May leaned in and whispered, "Are they not treating you right? Tell me. I'll get an inspector from county in here right away to fix any subpar conditions."

"Ah, this place is fine. I get potatoes with every meal. And I don't have to feel guilty about the carbs, because it's my only option."

Well, that explains a few things, I thought.

"We're doing our best, KP," I said. "And I'm keeping an eye on See-Saw for you."

"Yeah, that's great and all that you're looking after the little horse," KP said, "but I'm working on a tight timeline here. I'm going to Hawaii in six days! Remember?"

Miss May smacked her head with her palm. "You're leaving that soon!? KP. You need to get your money back."

"I don't think airlines and resorts have a refund policy for jailed vacationers," KP said. "It's not like someone died."

"Technically Linda Turtle died," I said.

"You know what I mean! I don't care about the refunds, anyway! I've been looking forward to this trip to Hawaii for years. It's the only state I haven't been to yet. I want to eat pig that's been cooked in the dirt. I want to see a volcano, get a fruity umbrella drink, and walk around with a lei and a t-shirt that says, 'I got lei'd in Maui.' You know all I get to drink here is a little tiny carton of milk? Umbrellas don't make sense in cartons of milk!"

"OK," Miss May said. "We're working on it."

"Work harder!"

The door to the visiting room clicked open. I turned,

hoping it wasn't Wayne. *Or was I hoping it would be him, shirt-less? Who can say?*

Either way, it was only Hercules, pointing at the clock on the wall.

"Time's up. That's it, Miller. Back in the cell."

Hercules waited as KP took his time standing up. KP yawned, stretched, and shuffled toward the exit, clearly messing with Hercules. When he finally got to the door, KP paused and shot a pleading look at me and Miss May.

"Please get me out of here."

Miss May and I nodded and assured KP we would do our best, then we said our "Alohas" and headed out to the parking lot.

Once we got outside, Miss May tossed me the keys to my pickup. "You drive for a while. I need to think."

"OK," I said. "Where are we headed? Home?"

"Not yet. I've got to pick up some dry-cleaning from Noreen, then we should probably brief Teeny."

"You got something dry-cleaned?" I asked. Miss May's usual uniform was a flannel and jeans.

"Noreen gave me a coupon," Miss May said. "Anyway, why are you so surprised? I have nice clothes."

"You have nice flannel and not-so-nice flannel," I said. "That's pretty much it."

"Just drive the truck," Miss May said.

I sighed and started the engine. I wanted to make progress in the investigation. And picking up dry-cleaning from Noreen was nothing more than a detour on our way to finding the killer.

Teeny grabbed our coffee cups and herded them all on

her side of the table. "If you don't stop investigating without me, no more free coffee! That's it!"

"We would have brought you along, but we're trying to keep a low profile," Miss May said.

"My profile is low, May! Come on. My name's not 'Teeny' for nothing!"

Miss May laughed. "You know what I mean."

"Yeah. You think I slow you down."

"I think...the cops have turned against us on this one. So we need to be careful," Miss May said.

"Can I have my coffee back?" I asked.

"You may not." Teeny turned to Miss May. "I am a valuable member of this sleuthing team, I'll have you know."

"I know, Teeny," Miss May said.

"I help! I gather information. Heck. You don't know. I might have information right now."

"Do you?" Miss May asked.

"Tell me I'm valuable."

"Teeny." Miss May rolled her eyes.

"Tell me I'm valuable. And beautiful. And young. I'm a teenage beauty sleuth!"

"OK," Miss May said. "You're a teenage beauty sleuth."

Teeny smiled. "Thank you. That's so sweet. But before I tell you what I know, I need you to tell me what you know."

"I know I want my coffee," I said. *One track mind.*

Teeny slid my cup back to me without looking away from Miss May.

"Fine," Miss May said. Then she recapped the case for Teeny with clipped brevity.

Reginald Turtle. Salazar the Psychic. Petunia the gambling flower shop lady. Ethel. Not that anyone suspected Ethel, but she did seem to be wrapped around Petunia's little green finger.

I listened as Miss May talked through our investigation, and my frustration mounted. The more she talked the clearer it became...we didn't have any solid leads. And every second we wasted meant another second KP had to spend in jail.

After three or four minutes, Miss May finished the recap. "Alright, T. Now you know what we know. So spit it out. What's the dirt?"

Teeny leaned forward. "OK. Ready?"

"Yes!" Miss May and I said in exasperated unison.

"Word has it, Reginald Turtle has been splashing money all over town. Shopping around for a new car. Extra-large lattes at the Brown Cow twice a day. He even came in here and ordered a deluxe appetizer sampler. Ate it all himself."

Miss May shrugged. "So? The Turtles are extravagant. That's their thing."

"I heard from a customer who shall not be named, who heard from someone else whose name I also can't say, who heard from someone else whose name I also can't repeat, that Reginald isn't spending any of the Turtle money. They were mostly broke anyway, and whatever's left goes to their son Herman or something. Reginald's spending life insurance money. The rumor is he took out a big policy on Linda. Recently."

I gnawed at my cuticle. "So Reginald got a big payday when Linda died? Like he had a financial incentive to kill her? In addition to apparently just not liking her very much."

Miss May nodded. "And didn't Linda mention that Reginald came from a less than wealthy family? He even took her name when they got married."

Teeny nodded. "That's the first thing she told me when I met them. 'Reginald's family is poorer than mine,' I think were her exact words. So it seems to me like he killed her to get some money for himself. That way he wouldn't have to share it anymore. Or put up with her nonsense."

Miss May lifted her cup to sip her coffee but paused halfway. "Why are you just telling us this now?"

"Mr. Turtle just started spending his dough last night. You want me to wake you up to let you know the new guy in town is eating too many appetizers?"

"That makes sense," Miss May said. "Probably takes a few days for insurance to pay out. Honestly, I'm surprised he got the money as quickly as he did."

Teeny shook her head. "I'm not sure he has the money yet. Gigley was saying Reginald had a problem with the insurance company."

"Gigley said that?" Miss May sat up a little straighter.

"He was in here earlier. I gave him some free pie, got him chatting," Teeny was practically bursting with pride.

"Why would Gigley have that information? Do lawyers deal with insurance companies?" I asked.

"All the time," Miss May said. "Especially when the circumstances surrounding a death are suspicious."

"Good intel, huh?" Teeny said. "Next time, make sure I'm involved from the beginning. I'll save you guys all that running around."

Miss May wiped her mouth and stood to go. "OK, then. Let's get going."

Teeny grabbed her sunglasses and put them on. "Woohoo! Wait. Where are we going?"

I grabbed my own sunglasses and put them on. "Yeah, where are we going? Do you want to talk to Reginald again or something?"

"Nope," Miss May said. "I've got a better idea."

14

SPECULATION AND SPAM

A s far as I knew, Tom Gigley was the only lawyer the town of Pine Grove had ever called its own. Miss May had retired before she moved from the city (*or was disbarred,* I thought darkly). His offices were housed in a converted colonial at the end of Main Street, and he had a little shingle hanging out front that said, "Law Offices of Tom Gigley."

Until a few months ago when I moved back to Pine Grove, I had never been to Tom's office. Gigley was an old friend of Miss May's, and she'd often left me to wander around town while she sorted out taxes or parking tickets or legal business about the farm in Gigley's office.

But after investigating three murders with Miss May, Tom's office had begun to feel like a second home to me. And Gigley, whom I had formerly known as the erudite, white-haired stickler in town, had emerged as a quirky oddball.

When we entered the office, Tom's secretary, Deb, was asleep, face down at her desk. For a split second, I worried she might be dead. I did have a knack for discovering dead bodies, after all. Then I heard a loud snore and breathed a sigh of relief.

Miss May pulled a homemade cookie from her purse and left it beside Deb. I smiled. *Classic Miss May, finding kindness in small moments.* I resolved to start carrying cookies in my bag and leaving them by sleeping citizens. *Probably not going to happen though,* I lamented. *If I carry cookies around, I'm just going to eat them all.*

Miss May, Teeny, and I chuckled as we tiptoed past Deb and made our way down the hall toward Tom's office. The door was open a crack, which was unusual. Every other time I had been there, the door had been closed, and Tom had been "with client." *Not that it ever stopped Miss May from entering.* But at that moment, he was sitting at his desk reading a document under a microscope.

Miss May sighed. "You need to get glasses, Tom!"

Tom looked up. "Will you leave me alone? What are you doing here?"

"I will not leave you alone. How will you do your job if you're blind? What is that you're reading with such tiny print, anyway?"

Tom lowered the paper. "If you must know," he said, "I'm reading a printed-out email. As you may recall, I had some issues with email earlier this year, so I took it off my computer. Now Deb prints out my messages, then I hand-write my replies, and give them to Deb so she can type them in and send them."

Miss May, Teeny, and I cracked up immediately. Teeny laughed so hard she had to grab a chair to steady herself. But Tom didn't even smile. In fact, the more we laughed, the redder his face became.

"That makes my millennium! Tom! You are a lawyer. You can't control yourself? You can't stop yourself from sending threatening emails to your cable provider?" Miss May took deep breaths between laughs, trying to get a grip.

Tom straightened his shoulders. "I decided it's not worth the risk."

Miss May stifled her laughter. "We're sorry. It's just...That is ridiculous."

"I'm not sorry," Teeny said, leaning against the chair.

"I'm glad I've entertained you," Tom said. "But if you're just here to laugh at me, I'd like you to leave. The last seven emails I've read were spam, and I need to keep going in order to find the message I'm looking for."

Teeny howled with laughter. "You print out the spam!?"

Tom crumbled the paper and threw it in the wastebasket. "Sometimes there are good deals!"

Tom stood up, fuming and tomato-red in the face. "What do you want!?"

Miss May, Teeny, and I took a moment to gather ourselves. Then Miss May spoke in a more serious tone. She explained that we were there to ask about Tom's dealings with Reginald Turtle. Tom refused to disclose any information. He wouldn't even tell us if Reginald was a client. Miss May wouldn't take no for an answer, but Tom was just as stubborn.

"I'm not asking for much," Miss May said. "Please. Just answer a few questions."

Tom shook his head. "You know I can't do that. You know better than anyone."

"I also know that you owe me, Tom. Or have you already forgotten? You would be in jail if not for Chelsea and me."

"Ahem," Teeny said. "What am I, dog poop?"

"And Teeny," Miss May amended.

"May, what you're asking me to do here could land me in jail again," Tom said.

"Only if I turned you in myself," Miss May said. "Tom. There is a killer out there. Yes. I am asking you to violate the trust of a client. I'm not proud of that. But I don't want you to carry the guilt if Reginald is a killer. Or if he kills again."

Tom looked up. Thought for a long moment. Finally he let out a sigh and relented. "OK. You have one question. Pick a good one."

Miss May took a moment, then asked her question...

"Did Reginald Turtle benefit financially from the murder of his wife, Linda?"

I stumbled out of Tom's office like I was emerging from a six-hour movie. We'd only been inside for a few minutes, but during those few minutes, I felt like I'd forgotten what trees looked like. The street seemed unfamiliar. The sun shone too brightly. I blocked my eyes with my hand, then remembered I had my sunglasses. Once my shades were on, things came into sharper focus.

"Well, Gigley basically just told us Reginald did it," I said.

"That's not true," Miss May said. "All Tom did was confirm that Reginald had taken the policy out on Linda."

"That's the same thing!" Teeny shook her head. "Men. Why are they all so greedy?"

I stopped walking as we reached the pickup. "That's not a fair assessment." *Or is it,* I wondered.

I hadn't had much luck with men. My experience with Mike, the fiancé from you-know-where, had been a waking nightmare. He'd abandoned me and stolen my apartment and my business. *So, OK, pretty greedy. But does one bad apple spoil the bunch?* An age-old orchard dilemma.

"Don't generalize, Teeny," Miss May said. "Some men are

great. Or so I've heard," Miss May tugged on the passenger door. "Chels. Unlock this thing?"

"Sorry," I said, as I unlocked the door. "Lost in thought."

"Time to get found," Teeny said. "This plot has gotten chunky."

"Do you mean 'the plot has thickened?'" I asked.

Teeny shook her head. "I said what I meant. We need a plan."

We climbed in the car. I put the keys in the ignition and turned to Miss May and Teeny. "So? Where to?"

"What do you think, May?" Teeny asked. "You're the lady Sherlock. Light up your corncob pipe and hatch a plan."

"Sherlock didn't smoke a corncob pipe," I said, then cursed myself for being such a know-it-all sometimes. *OK, all the time.*

"Oh, whatever," Teeny said. "Here's what I think, if anybody cares. Ready?"

"Ready," I said.

"OK," Teeny said. "I think Reginald took out the policy on Linda and then killed her so he could get the money. It's obvious, right? So let's go get him! Drag him out of that crummy old flower house kicking and screaming!"

Miss May rubbed her chin. "As much as I love that plan, I'm not sure we can do that yet. We don't have any evidence."

"Besides," I said, "if we're headed to see the killer, we should probably call the cops. Right?"

"Cops aren't going to help us on this one, Chelsea," my aunt reminded me. "Wayne's tired of us showing him up."

"Still," I insisted, "they'll come if we call. It's their job."

"And if we screw up? If we're wrong? We're off the case. And every case. Forever."

"Technically we're not even supposed to be on the case now," I said.

"But we are," Miss May replied. "And if Wayne catches us snooping and shuts us down, that means no one would be looking out for KP. They'll just bring him to trial and let the jury decide."

"I agree," Teeny piped up. "Who needs the cops? We're a vigilante crime-fighting force! Let's go Turtle hunting!"

"Uh. I don't love the sound of that." *For a few different reasons.*

Miss May waved me off. "Don't worry, Chels. We're not hunting anyone. We're just going to have a quick, casual conversation with Reginald about whether or not he murdered his wife to trigger an insurance payout."

Teeny rubbed her hands together, eager for action. "Kick this puppy into gear, Chels! We've got a mission!"

I turned to Miss May. "Do you really think we should talk to Reginald Turtle...without even notifying the police?"

Miss May shrugged. "We don't have much choice."

A roll of thunder shook the sky, and we all looked up.

"Better head out now," Miss May said. "Sounds like rain."

15

LATE SUMMER STORMS

As a kid, I had always loved playing in the rain, and I hadn't been afraid of anything. A few times, against the explicit instructions of my parents, I had even gone swimming during a thunder storm. Stupid, but fun.

I know better than that now, I thought. *It's a shame that living sometimes comes at the cost of feeling the most alive.*

As an adult, thunder storms made me nervous. And that afternoon, driving through a big storm on the way to Reginald's, my palms were so sweaty they slipped on the steering wheel.

I hunched over the wheel as I drove. And my eyes narrowed to slits as I struggled to see through the deluge. My wipers were in over their heads. And Miss May and Teeny's incessant chatting about Reginald Turtle wasn't helping.

"Can you two quiet down?" I snapped.

"Whoa!" Teeny laughed. "Is the new driver tense in inclement weather?"

"I'm not tense, but I can't see my hand in front of my face, so stop talking so much!"

Miss May laughed. "I think she's tense."

I made a glacial left turn onto Reginald's road. "Do you want me to crash?"

Miss May held up her hands in surrender. "Sorry. We'll be quiet."

I slowed as I approached Reginald's house. A tree had fallen in the street about 50 feet before his driveway, and there was no way around it.

"Great," I said. "What we do now? Should we try to move it?"

"No way!" Teeny said. "Make the town do it. That's why we pay taxes."

"I don't know that our tax dollars are going to work that quickly," I said. "What should I do in the meantime? Just park here, and we walk? We only have one umbrella."

Miss May smirked. "And it's so kind of you to lend it to your old aunt and her even older friend."

Teeny and Miss May strolled under their umbrella and laughed as I darted toward Reginald's house. At first, I hated the cold rain. But by the time I got to the driveway, I had completely forgotten my nerves, and I no longer felt tense or scared about seeing Reginald. *Maybe that's why I've always loved rain*, I thought. *Natural therapy.*

Either way, by the time I got to the porch, I was feeling bolder than my typical self. I rang the bell, even though Teeny and Miss May were still walking up the driveway. And I eagerly waited for Reginald to answer the door.

But he did not answer. I rang again. Still, nothing.

Miss May closed the umbrella as she and Teeny joined me on the porch. "Where is this guy?" Miss May asked.

Teeny peered through a front window. "Not home? In this weather?"

I shrugged. "Maybe he got caught in the storm."

"It's all dark in there," Teeny said. "Maybe we should break in. Troll for clues. I'll go find a rock!"

"We don't need to break in," Miss May said. "We're here to talk to Reginald, remember? Not steal his valuables."

Teeny sighed. "You can be so boring, May. What do you want to do then? Just sit here and wait?"

Miss May smiled. "Exactly."

When we got back over to the pickup, Miss May insisted that we remove the tree that had been blocking the road. Teeny resisted, demanding that we refrain in order to "get the most out of our tax dollars." But Miss May pointed out that there was nothing more conspicuous than sitting in a parked car right next to a fallen tree. And she had a point.

If anyone else came down that road, including Reginald, we would be a sitting truck. So, with much effort, grunting, and groaning, we dragged the tree over to the side of the road. By the time we were done, I was soaked to the marrow. But Teeny and Miss May managed to stay under the umbrella the whole time. *Don't ask me how.*

Twenty minutes later, we climbed back into the pickup, backed up 100 feet, killed the engine, and slinked down in our seats. Thus began our stakeout.

Five minutes into waiting, Teeny grew restless. She sat up and tapped Miss May on the shoulder. "You have any reading material?"

"No," Miss May said. "Besides, we're supposed to be watching."

"Ugh. How about snacks? Got anything to eat in your purse?"

Miss May shook her head. "Not today. Sorry."

Teeny huffed. "Come on! You always have something in that magical bag. Apple pie. Apple cookie. I'd even take just an apple if it's all you've got!"

Miss May held open her bag to prove that it was empty. Teeny flopped back in her seat with a pout. "Who goes on a stakeout without any snacks?"

"Technically," I said. "We didn't know this was going to be stakeout. Otherwise, believe me, I would've packed snacks."

Three hours later, there was still zero indication of Reginald, and the mood on the stakeout had turned hangry. The rain continued to fall. A howling wind rose from the east. And the three of us were going stir crazy.

"Are you sure we can't break in?" Teeny asked. "There has to be something we can learn in that house. And this guy isn't coming home. He's out partying with Linda's death fund!"

"Not a lot of midweek parties in Pine Grove," I said. "But it does seem like he might be out for the night. Maybe he went back to the city to be among his fellow Turtles? Or whoever his original people are." I turned to Miss May. "What do you think? Can we maybe try to go inside?"

Miss May rubbed her chin. "I don't know. If we get caught, the police are really going to be up our butts. We should probably play it safe."

"We've got a killer on the loose," Teeny said. "There's nothing safe about that. We've got to get in that house. Now."

"But Teeny, we can't—"

"No buts! I'm going in." Teeny jumped out of the pickup and stomped toward the house with her hands in her pockets.

Miss May followed. "Teeny! Slow down."

I hung back in the car for a few seconds, unsure. Although I was the one who had originally suggested going inside the house, I had also spent the previous three hours fighting the urge to start up my truck and drive home and not come out again until next summer.

So yeah...I had conflicting emotions.

But Teeny was forcing the issue. *Maybe that's what I needed*, I thought. So I climbed out into the angry night and ran back toward Reginald's house.

For the last time.

16

REGINALD'S RAINY DAY

I f you've never crept around the back of a suspected killer's house before, I wouldn't recommend it. Especially not if you're following Miss May and Teeny, whose chattering did not cease, even in the middle of a break-in in the middle of a storm. Those two were so distracted by the details of Reginald's house, they seemed to forget where they were.

"These window boxes are beautiful," Teeny said, as we edged down the side yard.

"I know," Miss May said. "Probably left behind from when Petunia lived here."

"I'm surprised she didn't take them with her," Teeny said. "Wouldn't put it past her."

Miss May clucked her tongue. "Poor Petunia. I feel bad she lost this place. She loved it so much. And look at the latticework along the roof. Gorgeous."

"Can we maybe stop talking for a minute?" I asked. "I'm damp and scared and we're breaking about a billion laws."

Miss May dismissed me with a wave of her hand. "Relax. Nobody's home, remember?"

We turned the corner and emerged into the backyard. A large pool had been sealed up for the season with a blue tarp. Moss obscured a beautiful brick patio. And a large barbecue rusted at the far end of the yard, rainwater dripping off its slipshod cover.

Petunia's old house looked beautiful from the back. There was more latticework and several sets of big glass windows. *What a shame that this grand old home had fallen on such hard times.*

A light on the very top floor caught my eye. I nudged Miss May and pointed. "Look. The whole house is dark, but there's a light on up there."

Miss May squinted up at the light. "Could be nothing. Reginald doesn't seem like he's super into energy conservation."

"True," Teeny said. "Or it could be...something." Teeny slowly turned toward Miss May. "We have to go check it out."

Miss May sighed and capitulated. "I suppose we could try to get inside."

"And if the cops catch us in there?" I asked.

Miss May shrugged. "We'll burn that bridge when we come to it."

"Cross," I muttered under my breath.

Miss May, Teeny, and I spread out along the back façade of the house to try to find an open door or window.

I tugged on a set of French doors over near the decaying grill, but they were locked.

After jiggling the handle several times, I cupped my hands and tried to get a look inside. But floral curtains, an obvious holdover from Petunia, obscured my views.

Snap! Crash!

The sound was so loud and calamitous, I lost my

balance, stumbled back, and slammed into the wall. Miss May rushed over to me.

"Chelsea! Are you OK?"

I looked around for the source of the crash. "What was that?"

Miss May chortled at my klutziness. "It was just a branch. See?"

Miss May pointed across the yard. A large branch had fallen from an oak tree and smashed into an outdoor table. The table had split in half like a karate-chopped cinderblock. I shook my head as I climbed to my feet. "Did we really have to do this during a storm?"

"Murder waits for no man," Miss May said.

"Hey! Over here!" Teeny whisper-shouted from the side yard.

When we rounded the corner toward Teeny, she was gone. My mouth immediately dried out with panic. "Teeny! Where are you? Are you OK?"

Teeny's little blonde head poked out from a nearby window with a big smile. "Better than OK. You guys have to see this place!"

Teeny disappeared into the house. Miss May and I exchanged a nervous glance. Then Miss May climbed into the window, and I followed, prepared for the worst.

I flopped inside after briefly getting my tummy snagged on the windowsill and landed with a thud on the hardwood floor.

Miss May helped me up, and I looked around. We were in a small but stately office, with 14-foot ceilings, an enormous built-in bookshelf, and a large oak desk shoved against the wall. Half the desk was covered in a painter's tarp, as was much of the floor. I also noticed a buzzsaw and some other tools propped against the wall.

"It looks like they were renovating this room," I said, speaking in a hushed whisper. "But it was already so beautiful."

"I have a feeling Linda Turtle liked to make everything her own," Miss May said. "But I agree. No wonder Petunia loved this house so much. Look at the moldings!"

Miss May was right. The moldings were ornate and quite large, with elaborate cornices at every joint. "They must be original to the house," I said. "I want to steal them."

Teeny tiptoed toward me. "Should we try to find that room that had the light?"

Miss May nodded. "And let's stay quiet in the rest of the house. I don't have a good feeling in here. You two ready?"

Teeny and I looked at one another and shrugged. *Not really.*

"Good," Miss May said. "Let's do this."

Teeny and I followed Miss May through the house like we were on a mission for Seal Team Six. Miss May pressed her body flat against the wall. Teeny and I followed suit. And we took gentle steps, careful not to creak the old floor-boards as we walked.

We tiptoed into a drawing room. A steepled ceiling rose twenty feet to a center point, and a grand piano dominated the far corner of the room, with sheet music propped on the stand. I crossed to the piano and saw the sheet music was for "Moonlight Sonata," by Beethoven. The song began to play in my head, an eerie soundtrack to our breaking and entering.

On the staircase, our gentle steps were useless. Every third step whined like a spoiled toddler. The whines evoked a rich history, a tapestry of children and parents traipsing up and down. *This is why I could never live in an old house*, I thought. *Too many memories trapped in the woodwork.*

We paused at the top of the stairs. Miss May and Teeny stopped to catch their breath. *OK, so did I.* Those stairs had been steep. Real steep.

I nodded toward a closed door at the end of the hall. A sliver of light emanated from the cracks. "That's the room."

Miss May held a finger to her lips to shush me. Then we began the long quiet march toward the lighted room.

The first room we passed on our way to the lighted room creeped me out beyond belief. A crib sat empty in the middle of the floor. Children's toys decorated a crumbling shelf. And the walls were painted an unnatural, creamy pink. Every few seconds, lightning strobed the whole horrific scene.

Linda and Reginald had mentioned having a son but he was in his twenties. And Petunia had grandkids but...what was up with this old Victorian crib? I wanted to point it out to Miss May, but I was too nervous to speak.

The next room on our right was weird in a totally different way. There was an elliptical machine. And some small weights. And a flat-screen TV, loaded with a "Work That Body" DVD. I recognized the muscular woman on-screen as a popular fitness guru. Her big, go get 'em smile and massive biceps chilled me to my core.

After what felt like eternity, we made it to the room at the end of the hall. Miss May looked at me and then at Teeny to make sure we were ready. We both shrugged like, "Ready as we'll ever be." The door was closed all the way, so Miss May had to turn the handle to enter. Well, she would have. But the door had no handle. *Spooky.*

Miss May nudged the door open with her shoulder and

took a step inside. Teeny grabbed my hand and didn't let go. We entered the room together.

And there was Reginald Turtle. Hanging from the ceiling fan.

Dead.

17

TURTLE NO MORE

I slapped my hands over my mouth to keep from screaming. Miss May froze. Teeny took a step back and thudded against the wall. "What the...?" Teeny's voice shook.

"I think..." Miss May couldn't get the words out.

"He's dead," I said. My voice was deep and guttural, as if it were coming from someone else's body.

An odd sense of calm washed over me. I was devastated that Reginald was dead, of course. But there had been so much tension in the moments leading up the stairs and down the hall. I had feared that Reginald might leap out and kill us at any moment. Now, to find him as we had, powerless to hurt us... *Well, it sounded cruel, but it relieved me.*

Reginald Turtle was the fifth dead body I had found since moving to Pine Grove. And this was the first time I had felt in control. Like I could find important clues and not just panic.

After getting over my initial shock, I scanned the room for anything out of the ordinary.

A sweater and trousers were hung in dry-cleaning bags

on the door. The bed was made with hospital corners, not a rumple to be found. The window had been opened, and a slight breeze blew the curtains back. In general, the place felt well-cared-for.

Would a man troubled enough to kill himself really have taken the time to make his bed with hospital corners? Maybe Reginald Turtle would have. But something felt wrong. Aside from the obvious man-on-the-fan.

"What are we doing?" Teeny asked. "Let's get out of here!"

"Doesn't something feel off about this?" I said.

"Yeah! The fan dongle is a dead guy," Teeny said. "I want to leave."

Miss May stepped toward the body. "Chelsea's right," she said. "Reginald doesn't strike me as the type to hurt himself. He seemed almost pathologically averse to discomfort." She turned to me. "Look. Fresh clothes from the dry-cleaner. And a well-made bed."

"The guy was a Turtle!" Teeny said. "You can't read too much into his neat-and-tidiness."

I kept searching the room for clues. "Did he leave a note?"

There was nothing on the bureau. Nothing on the writing desk. Then I noticed something sticking out of Reginald's shirt pocket. I pointed. "Look. That might be it."

Miss May cringed. "You want to take something out of his pocket?"

I shook my head. "I can't reach. I'm too short. So's Teeny."

Miss May grunted. Her height was being used against her.

"Somebody's gotta do it," I said.

Miss May squeezed her eyes shut. She muttered something to herself, presumably a preemptive request for forgiveness. Then she slowly reached toward Reginald's pocket. Just as she was about to grab the note, I pulled her arm away.

"Wait!"

Miss May's eyes shot open. "What? I was about to do it."

"You can't touch the note with your bare hand. Fingerprints!"

Miss May's face flushed. "Oh my goodness, you're right." She let out a deep breath, then she wrapped her hand in her shirtsleeve and reached up again.

Miss May extracted the note from Reginald's pocket with surgical precision. Teeny paced back and forth, moaning and groaning with nerves.

Seconds later, Miss May sat on the bed and unfolded the note.

Teeny bit her nails. "What's it say?"

Miss May cleared her throat and read aloud, "Dearest friends, family, loved ones, and citizens of my new home in Pine Grove: I, Reginald Turtle, have killed myself. If you are the first person to have the pleasure of reading this note, you have deduced as much already. Alas, I could not live with my guilt any longer. I confess to you, dear reader, that I murdered my wife Linda in order to cash in on a bounty of life insurance money. In truth, I have been planning to extinguish her for years. I regret that I waited until moving to this small town to finally handle my business. The people of Pine Grove are of hearty, peasant stock. They are a capable people, clearly. But they should not be forced to carry the burden of my crimes. It is a heavy burden, which I learned in the harshest way. Killing Linda was a scourge on my conscience and too much for me to shoulder. Please do not mourn me, for I mourned myself while I was alive. Also please send word to my son, German. Our little boy is an orphan now. And forever an orphan he shall be. Regards, Reginald Turtle."

Reginald's note cast a pall over the room. Teeny, Miss May, and I bowed our heads. Miss May reread the note to herself. After a long moment, she broke the silence. "His handwriting is beautiful."

I looked up. "What?"

Miss May chuckled. "Reginald has exquisite hand-writing."

Nerves jangling in my throat, I chuckled too. "That's what you have to say?"

"I'm surprised, that's all. It's lovely."

Teeny joined in with a chuckle of her own. "You are too much, May."

"Do you think he really killed Linda?" I asked.

Miss May looked back at the note. "I'm not sure. I'm not even sure he killed himself."

"Can we go!?" Teeny headed toward the door. "I'm spooked!"

Miss May took one last look around. "Okay. Let's get out of here."

"Hold on," I said. Teeny frowned and tapped her foot. "Hold on!" I repeated. I pulled my phone out of my pocket and snapped a few pictures of the room. It was a habit I had gotten into as an interior designer. It was always good to have a before picture, because otherwise the after pictures were less impressive. Though this wasn't exactly an analo-gous circumstance, I figured it couldn't hurt. A private collection of photos from the crime scene might come in handy later. Particularly because the police weren't exactly prone to sharing evidence.

I noticed a framed photo on the nightstand as I exited. It

was Reginald and Linda Turtle on their wedding day. Smiling, young, beautiful. *Like they had their whole lives in front of them.* I wondered, had they really been in love? How had that moment of happiness ripened into such bitter fruit? I thought about my own botched wedding, and I felt a flash of gratitude. Mike had humiliated me in front of everyone we knew, and it had felt like garbage, sure. But at least he hadn't trapped me in a union of slow-burning resentment.

Maybe I shouldn't be afraid of picking up his calls. Maybe I should talk to him. Maybe I should even thank him for what he did.

I glanced back at Reginald. I wondered if on their wedding day, Reginald and Linda could have possibly predicted how unhappy their lives would turn out. I had never met people so joyless. And, as was my wont, I turned to the dead guy and struck up a quick convo, "Sorry it ended up like this, Reginald. I hope...you and Linda aren't together, I guess, wherever you are."

Then, I hurried down the hall, down the stairs and outside...

Straight into the harsh lights of five parked police cruisers, waiting on the curb.

18

TRIPPING THE ALARM

Thunk. I walked straight into Wayne's brick-wall chest when I stepped out of the house.

"Chelsea. What are you doing here?"

Great question. Also important: does my hair make me look like a wet dog? If the answer is no, that's great. If the answer is yes, what breed of dog?

"Nothing," I said, like a five-year-old caught red-handed in the cookie jar.

"What do you mean 'nothing?'" Wayne said. "You broke into that home."

"Nu-uh," I said, still channeling my inner five-year-old.

"So Reginald invited you?" Wayne asked.

"Reginald's dead." The words were out of my mouth before I could figure out a more delicate phrasing. "If you didn't know that, then what are you doing here?"

"You tripped the silent alarm," Wayne said. He didn't seem to register the gravity of the situation. *Another Turtle has kicked the bucket!*

I glanced back at the house. Of course the Turtles had a

silent alarm. If they could have afforded it, they probably would have had a doorman and a butler, too.

"Hold on..." Wayne snapped to attention. "Did you just say that Reginald's dead?"

"Yeah...He, uh...he left a note."

"What kind of note? Are you talking about a suicide note?"

Suddenly, the weight of Reginald's death hit me like an anvil from the top of the Empire State Building.

A suicide note. A noose. A life snuffed out before its time.

I sat down on the front stoop.

"Chelsea. Did Reginald Turtle kill himself?"

I was speechless but managed a feeble nod from my perch. "It looks that way."

Wayne turned to his accompanying officer, the meek young Hercules. "Would someone stay with this girl? I need to go inside. Possible dead body. Potential suicide. Potential murder. Notify the coroner. Get some backup down here."

I looked past Wayne and saw Miss May and Teeny talking to the statuesque redhead, Flanagan. I found my voice. "No one needs to watch me."

"Somebody has to stay with you. You're a witness. And a possible criminal." Wayne turned away, but I impulsively stood and grabbed his arm.

"Wayne," I said.

He turned back. I didn't know what to say.

"Wayne," I said again. I wanted to accomplish so much with so few words. I wanted to tell Wayne that I was sorry, that we hadn't done anything wrong, that KP was innocent... And I wanted to warn him, tell him that he was about to walk into a horrible scene, that he would never be the same after this.

But I couldn't muster the courage to say any of those

things. So instead, I just stared into Wayne's eyes until Sunshine Flanagan approached.

"Miss Thomas?"

I turned to her.

"You need to come with me. We have some questions for you."

Miss May, Teeny and I spent the next hour talking to Flanagan and several other members of the Pine Grove Police Department. The officers had dozens of questions for us. But Miss May had been in plenty of high-stakes interrogations before. She knew what to say. And Teeny and I knew enough to stay quiet.

The cops accused us of breaking into Reginald's house. Fair enough. But Miss May was ready with an explanation.

"The back door was open," she said, cool as Salazar's cucumber water.

I hadn't realized it when we were inside, but Miss May had apparently unlocked the back door before we'd exited. Proof that the home was open.

The police pointed out that an open door did not give us the right to enter, but Miss May replied that she thought she had heard a commotion.

In a small town, hearing a commotion is tantamount to a presidential pardon. No matter what you've done or what the circumstances are, if you hear a commotion anywhere at any time, you have the right to investigate said commotion. People had wandered onto the farm during private events countless times, citing "commotion" as their reason for being on the property. It was impossible to argue with the commotion defense in Pine Grove, and even the police seemed to know that.

Miss May then told the police we had come to bring

Reginald a pie and an offer of our condolences for Linda. My aunt explained that we had rung the bell, but no one had answered. She went on to say that we had only gone inside to leave the pie somewhere safe, away from the rain.

The officers looked skeptical of Miss May's story. Flanagan, in particular, furrowed her otherwise flawless and uncreased brow. Detective Sunshine launched into a barrage of questions.

"Why did you go upstairs if you were only there to put the pie inside?"

"Why did you decide to deliver the pie during a torrential storm in the first place?"

"What kind of pie did you say it was?"

Miss May had an answer for every query, and she didn't miss a beat before a single response. Her calm demeanor and relaxed attitude impressed me. There was her inner lawyer coming out. *Or her inner-former-lawyer*, I thought, remembering Wayne's earlier accusation. Regardless of her current status with the New York State Bar, Miss May's steady answers placated Flanagan. I was grateful for that.

As we left, Flanagan warned us that there "might be more questions," and that "Detective Hudson might want to speak with us." But she let us leave, and that was good enough for me.

Miss May didn't speak much on the ride back to the orchard. Neither did I. Instead, I turned over the details of Reginald's death in my mind. I remembered the open window. The little pink bedroom. The eerie smile on the face of the DVD workout coach. And, of course, Reginald.

When we got home, I headed for the bathroom and a nice hot shower. I wondered if I could possibly scrub the bad feeling out of my brain. Miss May caught up to me before I got to the first landing.

"Shower?"

I nodded.

Miss May gave me a comforting smile. "I'll make hot chocolate. Come down after and we'll talk."

Looking down at Miss May from the landing, she seemed younger than usual. Childlike, even. And vulnerable. I smiled, hoping to offer some reassurance. Miss May smiled back, and I felt more adult than I had in a long time. Like Miss May and I were truly partners.

But as soon as Miss May plodded back to the kitchen to start the hot chocolate, I was left all alone on the landing. And standing there, hearing the silence of the old farmhouse, I felt twelve years old again. Tiny. Scared. And a little too excited for a warm bath and a big cup of cocoa.

I entered the kitchen with my hair wrapped in a towel, just as Miss May began to concoct her world-famous hot chocolate.

First, Miss May pulled a brick of locally-made dark chocolate from the pantry. She placed the chocolate on a beautiful maple cutting board and unsheathed her sharpest butcher knife from the chopping block.

Next, she slivered the chocolate into tight curls on the cutting board. A pile formed, 6-inches high. Like a chocolate Mount Vesuvius. After that, Miss May poured several cups of thick local milk into her favorite little red teapot and added a touch of heavy cream, "just to be safe." Once the milk heated up, she slowly added in the mountain of chocolate shavings and began to stir. After quite a bit of stirring, the chocolate blended into the milk, and the hot cocoa alchemy was complete.

Miss May then pulled out our favorite mugs — mine had a cat face on it and hers featured an image of the scales of justice — and she poured each of us a generous serving. She topped each cup with a mountain of homemade whipped cream. Then she used a cheese grater to dust a few more decadent chocolate shavings on top.

Finally, she slid me my mug with a small smile. "Here you go."

I took a slow sip and let out an involuntary, "Mmmm." Miss May smiled and indulged in a sip of her own. Then we got down to business.

"So," Miss May said. "We've got another dead body."

I nodded. "Not a fun development."

"Not fun at all." Miss May sipped her drink. "You think it was a genuine suicide?"

I shrugged. "I don't know. Reginald seemed so happy after Linda died."

"I agree," Miss May said. "Plus, the house was tidy. His dry-cleaning had been picked up. The bed had been made. Would you do all that if you were planning on killing yourself?"

"I don't do all that, and I'm planning on living until I'm 105," I said. I took a big sip of cocoa then let out a deep exhale. "So this is definitely another murder then."

"Not definitely," Miss May said. "But it's possible. Can you think of anyone who would have wanted Reginald dead?"

"Sure," I said. "He was almost as awful as his wife. But if someone murdered Reginald, I bet it was the same person who poisoned Linda's candy apple. Maybe it was one of the townspeople Linda and Reginald ticked off?"

Miss May shook her head. "Staging a suicide isn't the

action of an annoyed townsperson. It's planned. Not impulsive."

"So you think it was someone from out of town?"

"Or someone in Pine Grove who had a good reason to kill."

"And you agree that the same person killed both Turtles."

Miss May sighed. "I don't know, Chels. We need more information."

"What if the person who killed Reginald was after all that life insurance money he got after Linda's death?" I asked.

"The only person who would have a right to the money in the event of Reginald's death would be their son. And didn't Linda say that he's studying overseas?"

I nodded. "She did say that. Probably worth confirming?"

"His name was German, right?"

"Germany," I corrected. "So what's our theory right now? What do we know?"

Miss May grated some more chocolate onto her drink, and then mine. "Two theories. Number one: Reginald killed Linda and then felt so bad, he committed suicide."

"Number two?"

"The same person who killed Linda also killed Reginald. The killer was motivated by something primal. Greed, jealousy, envy, revenge. And whoever it is, he or she is still out there, running free."

I gulped down a sip of chocolate. "That's a scary way to say it."

I sighed. "So what do we do now? Do you think the cops will let KP out? If they think Reginald killed Linda?"

Miss May shook her head. "If we have doubts about the

suicide note, the cops do too. They're going to do some more digging before they let KP off the hook."

"That's so annoying," I said.

"Annoying but true," Miss May said. "We need to stay focused on solving this case. That's the only way we're going to help KP."

"OK," I said. "So what do we do first?"

Miss May tipped her mug back to get the very last sip. Then she set the mug on the counter with a clank.

"We find out if Reginald's death was really a suicide."

19

TEETER TOTTER, SEE-SAW

After a few more minutes of talking, Miss May asked for some "thinking space," and I was happy to oblige. There was so much going on. Linda's murder was unsolved. Reginald had committed suicide or been murdered himself. KP was still behind bars and in serious danger of missing his flight to Honolulu. I needed some room to think too. So I went out to see my old friend See-Saw, hoping she might help me find the clarity I desired.

It was around 9 PM when I trekked out to the barn. The night was unsettling. A chorus of crickets serenaded me from the dewy grass. An invisible owl hooted from a perch high in the dark trees. A low fog loitered among the shrubbery. The whole place seemed to whisper as I walked, and I didn't like it at all.

As I entered the barn, I spotted See-Saw neck-deep in a big bucket of apples. I assumed Miss May had come out to feed See-Saw recently because the bucket still had a lot of food left. I didn't want to interrupt See-Saw's dinner with a bunch of murder-chatter, so I slipped into the stall, sat down, and waited until she finished.

Watching See-Saw eat, a sense of stillness settled in my forehead and trickled down into my chest. Horses, with their placid eyes and soft demeanors, had always calmed me. Even though See-Saw was tiny, her presence was huge. And she had all the power to soothe me that a Clydesdale would.

Once See-Saw got close to the bottom of the bucket, I made a little small talk. "How about this weather?" "Seen any good movies lately?" "Those apples look good. Are they good? Are they nice and sweet?"

See-Saw kept eating, which clearly meant, "Yes, these apples are freakin' delicious, please shut up so I can eat." When the food was finally polished off, See-Saw looked up at me. I suspect she was hoping for more apples, but instead I started a conversation.

Over the course of the next half-hour, I reviewed the details of the case with See-Saw. I told her about Reginald and paraphrased his erudite note. I recounted the scene, and the haphazard renovations in Petunia's house. And I told her about the Turtles' son, and how he was an orphan. "I guess he and I have that in common, now," I said. "Parentless too soon."

For some reason, at that moment, I remembered how funny my dad looked whenever he wore a suit. His suits had never fit him quite right, and he'd rarely put one on. I thought about how he would have looked at my wedding, then I remembered that my wedding had been...incomplete. I felt a guilty sense of gladness that my dad hadn't gotten all dressed up for nothing. Then my thoughts meandered to Mike and his repeated attempts at contact.

"Have I told you how Mike keeps calling me?" I asked

See-Saw. See-Saw snorted. "I know," I said. "I should just pick up. I should talk to him. But I don't want to."

See-Saw shoved her face back into her apple bucket and licked up the juices. She didn't have time for my pointless boy drama.

"I'll call him back after we solve these murders," I said. "That's good, right? Don't you think? That would be a step forward?"

See-Saw continued licking the dirty bucket. "OK. Fine. I'll change the subject."

I looked around the barn, trying to think of something else for us to talk about. And that's when I noticed a spool of rope hung along a nearby gate.

The rope had been tied together with a crude knot. I assumed Miss May must have tied it after KP went to jail. KP had been a military man, and he would never stand for such sloppy rope work. Especially when it came to his best friend, See-Saw.

I stood up and gave the knot a gentle tug. It came apart in my hands without much coercing. And that was when I had a lightbulb of understanding.

"The knot!" I shouted.

See-Saw whinnied. My mind whinnied right along with her. Reginald's knot had been loose and wonky. Not at all secure. Maybe Reginald hadn't served in the military like KP had — Reginald didn't strike me as a wartime Turtle — but his ties had always been knotted with perfect double Windsors. Reginald had been a man who clearly cared about details. Plus, he had mentioned — repeatedly — that he owned three sailboats. *Didn't sailboat guys have an obsessive knowledge of knots?*

I turned back to See-Saw. "Reginald would never have tied such a bad knot. Not if he really wanted to...succeed."

Can horses shrug? If so, then that's how See-Saw responded.

"No," I said. "You don't understand. This is major. If Reginald didn't tie that knot, then he definitely didn't kill himself."

See-Saw nibbled at her haunch, still unimpressed by my revelation. But nothing could take the wind out of my proverbial sails.

But how could I prove that Reginald's knot was imperfect?

"The pictures! I took pictures of the scene."

I whipped my phone out of my pocket and unlocked it. There, in the photos, was an image of Reginald hanging from the ceiling fan. I didn't want to look, but I had to. So I zoomed in.

As gruesome as it was, I felt a thrill of satisfaction when I saw the knot. *I was right!* The noose had been tied with what looked like the knot on a little kid's scuffed up basketball shoes. Or on a Christmas gift wrapped with haste.

Reginald had been a serious man, and he took serious matters seriously. He wouldn't have rushed something like that knot. Besides, the knot in the photo was so loose I doubted it would've held Reginald's weight.

"See-Saw! What if someone killed Reginald and then tied the knot? What if hanging wasn't even his cause of death?"

See-Saw remained indifferent. But I knew my discovery was big. And Miss May needed to be informed.

I sprinted back toward the farmhouse. Then I stopped to walk. After about 100 feet I ran again, but that time it was more of a jog. Sure, I had just had an exciting breakthrough.

But that didn't mean that all of a sudden I could run a five-minute mile. Or a five-minute anything.

When I got back up to the house, I stopped to catch my breath, then I hurried up the stairs and pounded on Miss May's door.

"Yes?" Miss May called out, an edge in her voice.

"I had a breakthrough! Open up."

I could hear Miss May's grudging steps as she plodded toward the door. It creaked open and Miss May stood there, with her hands on her hips. She was wearing a long night-gown with a wide variety of apples on it, red and green and gold. I hadn't seen her in that nightgown for years, but I remembered giving it to her when I was a teenager.

Miss May had never been the easiest person to shop for. I never knew what to get her for holidays, but one year she had hinted that she wanted a t-shirt with apples on it. I had latched onto her suggestion, and every year since then I had bought her apple-themed attire. At this point, I knew she could never possibly wear all the apple garb I'd gifted her, but it was tradition, and we both liked it.

"What kind of breakthrough? I'm sorry, but I can't hear about Mike right now."

"This has nothing to do with Mike," I said. Then I added defensively, "But what if it did? You're done with Mike duty? I can't rely on See-Saw for all my advice, you know. She's smart, but she's no Miss May."

Miss May smirked. "We can talk about it at some point. But you know how I feel. I'm not the one you need to talk to." *She meant Mike.*

"Can I just tell you my breakthrough already?"

Miss May fanned open her palms, like "What are you waiting for?" and I launched into the revelation I had had about Reginald's knot.

At first, Miss May was skeptical. But I showed her the photos, and I reminded her of Reginald's sailing history and his affinity for Windsors, and yada yada yada. Eventually, Miss May got just as riled up as I was.

She paced. "Do you realize what this means?"

"Yeah," I said. "It means Reginald's suicide was definitely faked. And KP couldn't have killed him! We've got to tell Wayne."

"Chelsea! We are not involving the police in this investigation. Not now, and maybe not ever. I know you have a thing with Wayne..." *Do not!* "But the PGPD has proven largely incompetent and unwilling to cooperate."

I pushed my hair off my forehead. "So what does this mean then? What do we do now?"

"It means we can focus our investigation. If Reginald was definitely murdered, we can assume that Reginald and Linda were killed by the same person. Is there anyone we can think of who had motive to kill both Turtles?"

I sat down on the edge of Miss May's bed. The comforter had a big apple on it. That particular piece of apple kitsch was a gift from Miss May to herself. She had bought it ages ago, when the bakeshop at the orchard had really started to take off. The blanket was a reminder of her success. And it reminded me to concentrate on the million-dollar question.

"I can't think of anyone who would have wanted them both dead," I said. "Linda was much more hateful than him. And once she was gone, he seemed to really lighten up."

"Reginald wasn't quite likable either," Miss May said. "Together, they could have made some serious enemies."

"Maybe it was someone from out of town," I said. "An art dealer from Manhattan who they angered. A friend from a fancy cheese club, where they ate cheese every

Sunday until they felt sick. A turtleneck-wearing novelist who they joined twice monthly for a dinner of snails and flower petals?"

"Chelsea," Miss May said. "I get it. They were snobs. But I don't think they were murdered by a snail-eating fromager. I think they were murdered by someone right here in town."

"That's a new revelation," I said. "Who?"

Miss May sat on the bed beside me. "That's the question. But I refuse to believe it's a coincidence that they happened to get killed after moving here. I think they got killed <u>because</u> they moved here. Settling in Pine Grove was the catalyst for their deaths."

I rubbed my knees, which had been throbbing since my hundred-meter dash up to the farmhouse. As I rubbed, I looked around the room. I hadn't spent much time in Miss May's master suite since moving back to Pine Grove. She often referred to that room as her sanctuary, and she didn't love intruders. I wasn't exactly an intruder, but I wasn't exactly welcome company either. *Everyone needs privacy*, I reflected. So much of Miss May's home was part of a public space. All she wanted was this one room.

But it's such a nice room. Apple comforter. Apple curtains. Apple wallpaper. It was a lot of apple stuff, but it made so much sense in that room. As a kid, I had snuck into Miss May's room sometimes when she was out working. I loved all the little details of her space. Especially the door handles.

One year for Christmas, KP had made her wooden door-knobs shaped like apples and installed them for her. Miss May had insisted that the little oak apples were "too much" and that she was going to seem like "a crazy apple lady." But we could all tell that she loved the doorknobs. Sometimes little touches like that really made a house feel like a home.

And just like that, another lightbulb smacked me in the face.

"The doorknobs!" I yelled. *I should really work on modulating my voice.*

"Whoa, Chels," Miss May said. "What about them?"

"Did you notice that doorknobs and fixtures were missing at Reginald's house?"

Miss May stood and tidied little odds and ends as we talked. "Yeah, I noticed. Part of the renovations, I assumed. What's your point?"

"Did you also notice how nice the fixtures were at Petunia's apartment? Way nicer than the stuff that comes standard at the typical 55 and older community."

"That's a luxury resort community." Miss May emphasized luxury as if the adjective explained Petunia's antique fixtures. But it didn't explain anything.

I stood up. "I worked on a place like that. Helped design the clubhouse. The word luxury refers to the amenities. The pool. The tennis courts. The farmhouse sink in the communal space. The apartments themselves were very basic. I made a few suggestions to the developers, but they insisted on 'standardized' finishes for every unit."

"When did you work on an old folks' home?" Miss May asked.

"Early on. It wasn't a great job, but I needed the experience. Whatever, that's not important!"

Miss May stopped tidying and looked at me. "So you think Petunia...What? Stole the fixtures from her own house and had them installed in her little old lady apartment?"

I shrugged. *Would that really be so crazy?*

"That's crazy, Chelsea. And I didn't see any signs of a break-in. Did you?"

"She could have climbed into the same window we did."

Miss May shook her head. "Petunia has two titanium hips and only half a knee. I doubt she would have made it through any windows."

I scratched my head. "OK. Well, what if she still had a key to the house? That's not out of the question. The Turtles might not have changed the locks. Or maybe they left a door open at some point."

"I don't know," Miss May said. "How do you even know that the fixtures in her apartment were from the Turtle's house? Petunia loves nice things. Maybe she bought those knobs and fixtures at an antique shop or something."

"I might be more inclined to believe that...if the Turtles had doorknobs on their doors. But the two things together? That's too much of a coincidence."

Miss May nodded. "I suppose she could have entered with a key. But it's quite a stretch to go from stealing your own antique doorknobs to staging suicides and killing people in cold blood. Plus, do you think Petunia sat there and forged a suicide note? It was so...detailed. And dramatic. And it sounded a lot like Reginald had written it."

"You agree that the knot proves Reginald was murdered, right?" I didn't wait for Miss May to answer. "So somebody wrote that note. Or they forced Reginald to write it before they killed him."

"Petunia is almost a hundred years old. I just don't know if she still has that much spunk left in her."

"You've seen her play cards! She's basically all spunk! And she never provided an alibi."

"I guess I could see Petunia getting violent," Miss May reasoned. "She did practically throttle Ethel over a stupid poker game, and that's a lot less personal than a treasured family home."

I stood up, feeling increasingly confident. "Exactly!

Petunia is a real suspect." I stepped toward the door and turned back to Miss May. "Let's get out of here."

Miss May laughed. "I told you. You can't get into Washington Village this late at night."

I groaned. "Not even for something like this? You know everyone. Bring them a pie! Charm them! It's not even 11 PM."

Miss May shook her head. "They lock that place down like a fortress. We'll go in the morning."

I sighed. "Fine. First thing tomorrow." I watched as my aunt, a woman who had been a pillar of all things good and true and moral for my whole life, tucked herself into her covers. And suddenly, I had to ask her something. The words were out before I could reconsider. "Miss May...What did Wayne mean when he said you weren't a lawyer anymore?"

Miss May scoffed. "That man doesn't know what he's talking about."

Her answer was noncommittal, but her tone was definitive. She wasn't going to elaborate, and there was no point pressing her on the issue.

"OK," I said. "See you in the morning."

20

FIXTURE FIXATION

The next morning we left at 7 AM to go talk to Petunia. First, we checked in with the guard. He was friendly, as per usual. And we didn't even have to wake him up to get through the gate that time. He handed us the huge sign-in book and Miss May obediently scrawled her name on the skinny line provided for guests.

Then we headed straight to the clubhouse. No surprise, we found Petunia 20 hours deep in a poker game with her card shark friends. *Maybe this is why they lock down Washington Village after dark*, I thought. The place had the vibe of a seedy underground casino in Chinatown. Only replace sleazy men and Russian criminals with little old ladies, of course.

Petunia groaned as Miss May and I approached. "Go away! I don't know you. I don't want to know you. Don't you know better than to interrupt a magnificent streak?"

Petunia's gruff rebuke was almost enough to make me hightail it back home. The florist scared me. But Miss May was not so easily deterred. "Great to see you again too, Petunia. Can we grab you for a second?"

I had a strong sense of deja-vu as we cajoled and wheedled and sweet-talked to try and get Petunia to rise from the table. But that time, Petunia would not get up from her chair, nor would she speak to us in front of the other ladies. "Not until I double my money or lose it all!"

We decided to wait. Miss May and I hunkered down in a pair of folding chairs along the wall. As the game went on, fewer and fewer women stayed at the table. Each time one of the ladies got up, Petunia shamed them. "Looks like you're a loser after all, Geraldine!"

Or she'd cut even deeper, with a personal insult like, "No wonder your son can't hold a job. His mother's a quitter!"

Every time Petunia lashed out at one of her table mates, I side-eyed Miss May. I had never conceived of an elderly woman who seemed more capable of murder. Petunia had a mean-streak, and she wasn't shy about it. *Plus, she had an inexplicably creepy crib in her old house. Shudder.*

Eventually, Petunia was left alone at the table with poor, meek Ethel. They played heads-up Omaha high-low split, whatever that was. Petunia seemed eager to face off against a weaker opponent, and Ethel was no match for Petunia's aggressive style of play.

Moments into the game, Ethel ran out of cash and sadly shuffled toward the exit. But Petunia wouldn't let Ethel go quietly. Just as Ethel reached the door, Petunia called out. "Ethel! Sweetheart. Wait a moment."

Ethel turned back, not willing to meet Petunia's gaze.

"Look at me. Look at me when I'm talking to you." Petunia's voice had a cruel edge.

Ethel looked up and met Petunia's eyes.

Petunia smiled. "If you're going to the deli, I need a pound of Swiss. Sliced thin, okay sweetheart?"

Ethel exited with a subservient nod. Then, at long last,

Miss May and I had our opportunity to have a private conversation with Petunia.

Petunia didn't look up from counting her winnings as we approached. "You two are still here? Wow. Pathetic. Chelsea, don't you have a man in your life? At the very least I'd expect you to have a golden retriever that enjoys your company."

"I have a tiny horse," I said. "See-Saw. She and I get along great." *Why am I justifying myself to this woman?!*

Miss May laughed. "Oh come on, See-Saw isn't even your horse. Honestly, Chelsea. Petunia is right. Aren't you tired of tagging along with me? It's a little sad."

Ouch! My lower lip protruded, and I pouted like a slapped fish. "What... what do you mean it's sad?"

Miss May looked at me and winked. *Ah. It was an act. But why?* Miss May turned back to Petunia. "You see everything exactly as it is, Petunia. I've always respected that about you. You don't mince words."

Oh. Miss May was using me to bond with Petunia. Miss May thought that if she put me down, Petunia would warm up a little. It might have been a little mean, but it was a solid strategy. And it seemed to be working.

Petunia sneered at me. "See what you're doing, Chelsea? You're making two sweet old ladies sad. "

Petunia laughed, and Miss May joined in. Even though I knew Miss May was just playing into Petunia's hand, I had to resist the urge to defend myself.

"So," Petunia said. "You waited to talk to me for four hours. Why are you here? You want me to teach you the secret to Omaha high-low? 'Cuz I'm taking that to my grave!"

Miss May shook her head and leaned forward. "Actually. We're still working on that Linda Turtle case. We don't have any leads, and we thought you might be able to help."

Petunia bristled. "I told you before, I didn't know those people. And I didn't blame them for stealing my house. They seemed like real dung beetles, but I don't know anything about them."

"You didn't see them poking around your house at all before they bought it? I heard they were snooping around the property before the foreclosure was even official." *News to me.*

Petunia shook her head. "No. The foreclosure all happened pretty fast. Made my head spin." Petunia tilted her chin up, her nose in the air. But I could tell, talking about her lost home tugged at her rusty old heart strings. I felt bad for her, but I also felt like I was seeing "motive" written all over her upturned nostrils.

"I see," Miss May said. "So you never even talked to the Turtles before they took over your house?"

"I told you," Petunia snarled. "No."

Miss May tried to cool things down. "OK, I'm sorry. I'm just—"

Petunia stood up. "All right. I'm done here. Time to go back home and take my medicine. Ethel should be back with my thin-sliced Swiss pretty soon."

Petunia scooped handfuls of money into her purse. Miss May watched, her lips pressed together in frustration. I could tell that Miss May was having trouble working around to the subject of the fancy fixtures, our only big clue, so I jumped in.

"Petunia, I meant to tell you before. I loved the fixtures in your apartment."

Petunia froze. She looked up. "What's that supposed to mean?"

I shrugged. "Nothing. Just wanted to pay you that compliment. The light fixtures. The cabinet handles. The doorknobs. They look antique. Like they came from an old Colonial manor."

Miss May glanced at me. I couldn't tell if she was happy or annoyed. My tactics were far from subtle, but I didn't want Petunia to escape.

When I look back at Petunia, she was leaning on the table for support. All the air seemed to have left her body, and she looked like a deflating balloon.

"Are you okay?" I inquired.

Petunia croaked out her next words with difficulty. "Those were my fixtures. I remember the weekend my father installed them. He had spent all his money, every nickel and dime of his savings, building that house. For my mom and us kids. It took years. When we moved in, me, my two brothers, my sister, and my mom, he didn't have any money left for the finishing touches. The place was rough around the edges. Doorknobs? Forget about it. We didn't have doors. At first, my mother was upset. She wanted to live in a real, complete house. But I loved it. The place was so open. We were all together then. No doors, nothing between us. After we had been living there two years, maybe three, my dad saving up the whole time, he came home with the most beautiful brass and copper pieces money could buy. I didn't want our home to change at first. But watching him install all these fixtures, I understood pride. I understood hard work. I understood what it means to live in a place that's yours."

Petunia trailed off. She waved the memories away, like she had been silly to relive them. "Anyway. Yeah, I stole them. Good job, Watson. So what? You want to throw me in prison for rescuing my father's fixtures from those awful reptilian devils? Go ahead. They've got poker in jail."

Miss May and I exchanged a worried look. Then Miss May turned to Petunia. "I don't think you'd go to jail for taking the fixtures but...you could tell us. If you got angry. If you, perhaps, did something else."

Petunia straightened. "Something else? You think I snuffed those Turtles out? What kind of monster do you think I am?"

"You misunderstand, Petunia," Miss May said. "I don't think you're a monster. I think plenty of people would be furious in your situation."

"Don't try to weasel a confession out of me, May! Those fixtures are my proof I didn't kill those wretched Turtles. I was at the house stealing those knobs and lights while you were having your little candy apple party. That's where the woman died, right?"

"That is where she died, yes," Miss May pressed on. "But can you prove you were at your old house during that party?"

Petunia laughed. "Unbelievable. Yes. I do have proof. Ethel was my getaway driver."

"Ethel can drive?" *Foot, welcome back to my mouth.*

"She's an excellent driver, I'll have you know," Petunia said.

I had to suppress a laugh at the mental image of Ethel speeding away with Petunia and a bunch of pilfered doorknobs.

"Ethel would confirm this story if we talked to her?" Miss May asked.

Petunia shrugged. "Sure. Good luck, though. She can't hear, and she doesn't listen."

"You know what?" Miss May said. "We've caused enough trouble. We don't have to talk to Ethel right now. We'll see ourselves out."

"Good. Do that." Petunia resumed shoveling her winnings into her purse, and Miss May and I walked away.

As soon as Miss May and I got out of earshot, I had a million questions. *Why didn't we force Petunia to show us real proof? Why hadn't we pressed her about Reginald? Why weren't we on our way to talk to Ethel?*

But as usual, Miss May had a plan. She charged straight to the guard station at the entrance. "We're ready to check out," Miss May said the man. He nodded and handed my aunt the check-in book.

Miss May took the book and walked straight to the car. Then she got in, and we drove away.

21

FARM TO TABLE

A s soon as we exited Washington Village, I leafed
through the big book, looking for a clue. If
Petunia had checked in or out the night Linda
died, that would tell us a lot about whether or not she could
have committed the murder. Obviously, Petunia could have
snuck out if she'd really wanted to, but this book could still
have a clue.

Just as I was about to flip to the page with the dates in
question, Miss May's phone rang. "Teeny!" Miss May said as
she answered. "You got us just as were about to find an
important clue. Or not. Not sure yet."

A voice came over the line, shrill and excited and Teeny
in every way. Miss May laughed.

"OK. OK. We won't open the book until we get there."
Miss May looked at me and shrugged.

"Miss May! Are you kidding?"

Miss May hung up with Teeny and turned to me. "It's
just a few minutes. Relax."

I was so eager to peek in the book, the "few-minutes"

drive felt like it took six lifetimes. Then, after an inter-minable trek, we finally arrived at Teeny's restaurant.

When we entered Grandma's, the place looked more formal than it ever had. White tablecloths were on every table. Fancy China decorated each place setting. And clas-sical music drifted out of the speakers, replacing the usual Patti LaBelle.

Teeny approached, wringing her hands. "Hey! What took you so long?"

"Time slowed down," I muttered.

"Forget about that," Miss May said. "What the heck happened in here? It looks like you serve fine French cuisine. And what are the waiters wearing? Are those tuxedos?"

Teeny giggled. "I told Petey he could take over the restaurant for the rest of the week. Remember how he wants to be a chef now? You have to support these kids in their dreams."

"That's nice," I said. "But what's with the tuxes?"

"Ah, they're just t-shirts that look like tuxes," Teeny said. "Petey wants to do an upscale thing."

Miss May shook her head. "Have you thought this through, T? The people of Pine Grove tend to feel uh, alien-ated when things are too fancy."

"You think I don't know the people in this town?" Teeny asked. "I'm supporting Petey. I told him all about what people in Pine Grove want. But he insisted. So I'm going to let him learn that lesson the hard way. Freed up the rest of my week to investigate with the two of you."

I smiled. "Ohhhh. You let him do this because you want to sleuth around town. You're not supporting him!"

"Can't I do both?" Teeny asked.

Miss May and I laughed, just as Petey rushed passed us

carrying a sad-looking soufflé on a silver platter. He was sweating nuclear warheads. And he almost slipped in his own perspiration as he rushed to deliver the soufflé to Humphrey, one of Teeny's elderly regulars.

We watched as Humphrey received and then poked at the soufflé, casting a suspicious glance up at Petey.

Teeny leaned in to me and Miss May and whispered, "I told Petey that Humphrey likes fancy cheeses and exotic cuisine. Truth is, Humphrey hasn't eaten anything other than pancakes since Vietnam!"

We watched Petey and his staff serve a few more odd-looking dishes, then Teeny led us over to our favorite booth in the restaurant, and we got down to business.

"OK," Teeny said. "What's up with this investigation? What's the big new clue?"

Miss May held up the guest book that she had stolen from Washington Village. "Voila!"

Teeny grabbed the book and opened it. She thumbed down the ledger lines and leaned in to get a close look. She muttered to herself as she read.

"Uh, Teeny," I said. "Do you know what you're looking for?"

Teeny looked up. "Of course I do!"

"And?" Miss May prodded.

"OK, fine, I don't know," Teeny tossed the book down. "What is this book?"

"It's the check-in and check-out book from Washington Village," I said.

Teeny nodded. "Oh. In that case what I see is that old people go out later than I thought."

"You're technically old enough to live in Washington Village, you know," Miss May said.

"Age is just a number," Teeny said. "And numbers don't

matter to me. Unless they're followed by the words 'percent off.'"

Miss May reached out and took the book from Teeny. "Let me see that. We're looking for the records from the date Linda Turtle was murdered."

Miss May flipped back a few pages. Then she pointed. "Here it is!" Miss May put on her glasses to get a better look. She thumbed down the ledger, just as Teeny had.

"Do you see anything?" I asked, impatient to learn the book's secrets. "Did Petunia check herself out on the night that Linda died?"

Miss May took off her glasses. "Petunia did check out that night."

Teeny gasped. "So that sweet little flower lady is a killer?"

"She's not sweet," I replied.

"Keep it down," Miss May said. "I didn't say Petunia did it. In fact, the opposite could be true. This might be Petunia's alibi. Petunia told us that she went out that night. She claimed that she broke into the Turtles' house and that she was there at the time Linda was killed."

Teeny rubbed her eyes. "So Petunia's alibi for not killing Linda is that she was breaking and entering? That's not ideal for her."

"It's worse than that," I said. "This evidence here? The check-in books? It doesn't prove that she was at the Turtles' house at all. It only proves that she went out the night Linda was killed. That's not an alibi. It's almost incriminating."

"It would be incriminating. Except for one important detail," Miss May said.

"What do you mean?"

Miss May handed me the ledger. "Take a closer look."

I reviewed the page, looking for a clue. Miss May

smirked as she watched me. She seemed to take pleasure in my confusion.

"The answer is right there in front of your face, Chelsea," Miss May said. "If someone checks out that means they have to..."

"Check back in!" I looked at the opposing side of the page on the ledger. There, in black and white, was the check-in page for the night that Linda was killed. I scanned the names on the list and stopped when I came to Petunia.

"She checked back in before the hoedown even started! There's no way she could have been at that party to kill Linda."

"Unless she poisoned the apples earlier that day," Teeny said.

Miss May shook her head. "Not possible. The apples hadn't been made until that afternoon and Petunia was not on the orchard. We would have seen her. The apples never left my or KP's sight between the bakeshop and the event barn."

"But somebody poisoned Linda's apple," I countered.

"It had to be later on, once the apples were in the barn," Miss May said.

Teeny let out a sigh of relief and wiped the back of her hand against her forehead. "Thank goodness, Petunia isn't a killer. I couldn't sleep at night if I knew all the floral decorations I had ever bought had been arranged by a psychopath."

"Hold on," I said. "What about on the night of Reginald's death? Had Petunia checked out then?"

Miss May held up a finger and flipped through the pages of the book. She stopped after a few pages and scanned with her thumb again. Teeny and I watched on the edge of our proverbial booth seats.

"She was home all night," Miss May said. "Didn't go out or in."

"Probably stayed holed up in that weird little flower den she's got," Teeny said. "That place gives me the creeps."

"You haven't even been there!" I said.

"But you told me about it," Teeny said with a shudder.

"Well, she was probably gambling all night in the club-house anyway," I said.

"Of course," Ms. May said. "That's always a possibility."

Teeny crossed her arms over her chest. "Hold on a second! Petunia's still playing cards down at the clubhouse? She told me they banned poker, and nobody plays anymore!"

Miss May and I exchanged a look.

"No comment," Miss May said. "Besides, we have a bigger problem to solve right now."

"What problem could be bigger than me getting kicked out of that poker game? I loved those all-nighters! Plus, I always won."

"And I think we've just discovered why you stopped getting invited to the games." I said.

"Those little old ladies were easy money!" Teeny said. "It's not my fault they don't know how to play."

"Can we focus on the double murder we're investigating?" Miss May said. "Not that we're not interested in hearing about your poker skills, but maybe after we catch the killer."

Teeny smiled. "Deal. But you should know now. I never lost. I did get in a couple of fist fights, though."

"Who won in those?" I asked, disturbed.

"Who do you think?" Teeny replied with a devious smile.

I shrunk back in my seat.

"Oh, I'm just kidding," Teeny said. "You know I'm not a

fighter! Now let's talk about new suspects. I think it was probably a secret stepfather that Linda had never met. And the stepfather just came back from a trip sailing across the world. And Linda had stolen some gold that the stepfather had left to Linda's bedridden mother. And he wanted it back!"

Miss May sighed. "That's an episode from the *North Port Diaries,* isn't it?"

"Does it matter?" Teeny asked. "It's a legitimate theory. It could happen! Those ideas are ripped from the headlines in that show. It's all based on real-life, you know."

"OK," Miss May said. "Let's make a note of the 'stepfather hunting for gold after traveling the world on a sailboat' theory. Great idea. Is there anyone else we can think of who might have had a motive to kill both Linda and Reginald?"

I shrugged. "We have no idea. But Miss May thinks it has something to do with them moving back to town. Pine Grove was somehow the catalyst for their murders."

"Actually, I've revised that theory," Miss May said. "I have a new number one suspect now."

"You do?" I asked.

Miss May smirked.

"What the heck? When were you going to tell me?"

"I just came up with it now," Miss May said. "But I don't need to tell you. You've got all the information. You just need to think about it."

"And we're sure it's not a secret step-dad," Teeny said.

"Hold on, Teeny. Let me think for a second." I closed my eyes and ran over the details of the case...

Who from the Turtles' past did I have any awareness of? And which of those people would've wanted both Turtles dead? The Turtles had money, and money often equaled motive. But motive for whom?

"Their son!" I gasped. "Germany. What if he is the beneficiary of their wills? They would both probably need to die in order for him to see that money. I doubt they'd let go of their dwindling fortune if one of them were still alive."

"But Linda said that kid was studying in Africa or something," Teeny said. "Getting a PhD in professional snobbery. She told everyone in town."

"That's what the Turtles told us," Miss May said. "But what if they were lying?"

Teeny's eyes lit up. "Ah! You're right! Maybe Germany Turtle is a slob. He lives in Jersey City like Chelsea did when she was a slob. But Linda and Reginald pretend he's in Africa so they don't have to admit his slobbiness to their socialite friends! Or maybe Germany has a bungled-up face, so they lie and say he's in Africa when really he's in a mental institution right here in America. Maybe he's been simmering with rage all these years, and he finally snapped and killed them for revenge and to get all their money!"

"That's kind of what I'm saying," Miss May said. "Maybe slightly less *North Port Diaries* but...along those lines."

Teeny stood up. "So let's go find him! Where does he live?"

"...Africa?" I said. "At least as far as we know."

Miss May shook her head. "But I bet he has a residence here in the States. And he's probably back right now, since both of his parents have turned up dead. But I have no clue how we're going to figure out where he is. Should we go to the library? Try to find a phone book or something?"

I held up my phone. "I found him. He has a house in the Hamptons. Most likely one of the Turtles' vacation homes."

Miss May looked shocked. "That was amazing. How did you do that so fast?"

"It's not forensics or anything. I Googled him. You may

be surprised, but there are very few 'Germany Turtles' in the tristate area."

"All right," Ms. May said. "It looks like we're headed to the Hamptons."

Someone cleared his throat nearby. I looked up to see Petey standing above us with a silver platter just like the one he had brought Humphrey earlier.

"Ladies. It is my pleasure to serve you this afternoon."

"Oh, uh...we didn't order anything," Teeny said.

"This dish is compliments of the chef," Petey said. "Turkish figs over baby lettuce heads, marinated carrots, frilled mustard greens, and caramelized leek sprouts. Served with hand-torn mozzarella and cylindrical beets. All topped with a seared apple reduction. And served with fresh-cut, sea-salt French fries."

"Yum! Fries!" Teeny grabbed a handful and shoved them in her mouth. "Can you toss the rest in the fridge? We've got to go."

Petey looked horrified. "This cuisine is meant to be served fresh! You can't put this masterpiece in the fridge like common leftovers!"

"I'm still your boss. So yeah. You can." Teeny slid out of the booth and headed for the door. Miss May and I also grabbed a couple of fries and followed after Teeny.

"It looks great, Petey," I said, even though it looked pretty weird.

Petey called out as we left. "This is fine cuisine! Where are you going?"

As soon as we were out of earshot, Teeny turned to us and laughed. "That kid is too much."

"These fries are good though," I said.

"They're amazing," Teeny said. "I'll have to get him to bring me some of that fancy salt."

22

LONG ISLAND BOUND

Although I had almost half a tank of gas, Miss May forced me to stop and fill up before we left town.

"You never know how much gas you're going to need on the way to Long Island," she said.

"She's right," Teeny said. "The Long Island Expressway is interminable. It's designed to get you all turned around and confused."

Miss May nodded. "I once spent 15 hours going from Pine Grove to East Hampton for a wedding."

"Did you make it to the wedding in time?" I asked.

Miss May shook her head. "And it was especially bad because I was catering desserts."

"OK, OK, I'll get gas," I said. "We're here, right? I'll go inside to prepay."

"And get snacks," Teeny said. "Something with sprinkles."

"I don't think the gas station sells snacks with sprinkles," I said, one foot out the door.

"Would it kill you to look? All I've had today are samples of Petey's weird stick food."

"That food looked great," I said, messing with Teeny. "I think people in town will love it. Could put Grandma's out of business."

"Just get me some sprinkles!"

I laughed and hopped out of the car, crossing toward the snack shop. I mean, gas station.

Moments later, I was perusing the snack options, running my hand along a variety of honey buns and peanuts and apple pies, when my mind wandered to thoughts of Detective Wayne Hudson.

I had spent much of the last week angry at Wayne. He had jailed KP for no reason. OK. Maybe he had some reason, but he hadn't even talked to me about it first. He had lost all respect for me and Miss May. And as far as I could tell he had made no progress on the murder investigation, despite having police resources at his disposal.

Still, Wayne had a certain *je ne sais quoi*, and I wanted to sais quoi. I didn't usually go for a typical manly type — Mike was scrawny and meek — but something about Wayne's massive frame and general gruffness appealed to me. *OK, he was handsome. And funny. And he was standing right in front of me.*

Wait! What?

Yup. It was as if I had summoned him with my mind.

"Do you need help carrying that stuff?" Wayne asked.

I looked down. I hadn't even realized how many snacks I'd collected. In my arms were five packs of spicy tortilla chips, several candy bars, two sodas, three turtle doves and a partridge in a pear tree. I had the snacks cradled in my arms like a newborn baby, which made the whole thing even sadder.

"I'm good," I said, fumbling with my armful of treats.

One of the candy bars slipped from my swaddle of

snacks and hit the floor. Wayne picked up the candy, glancing at me with a smile. He wasn't wearing his suit that day, nor was he displaying his badge on his belt as he often did. Instead, he wore a flannel shirt with blue jeans and muddy brown boots. He looked strange out of his normal uniform, but I liked it. It was like an alternate reality Wayne.

"Are you headed to a party or something?" Wayne asked, eyeing my snacks.

I laughed. "Oh yeah. It's a uh, kegger. Me and Miss May and Teeny. We get pretty crazy."

"Don't get too rowdy. I'll have to issue you a citation."

I crossed to the counter and plunked my snack collection down. Arthur, the rotund older man who worked the cash register, looked shocked by my bounty.

"That's a lot of snacks, Chelsea! Are you sure you want all that for yourself?"

"It's not just for her," Wayne approached from nearby. "She's having a wild bash with her aunt and her aunt's friend."

"Looks like a lot of food even for three people," Arthur said.

"We're not going to eat it all, Arthur. We like to have a little bit of everything. And you should really get something in this place that has sprinkles. There's a high demand for sprinkles in this town, and you're not meeting it."

Arthur narrowed his eyes. He didn't seem to appreciate my sprinkle tirade. "That'll be $9.95."

I handed Arthur my credit card. He pushed it back. "Can't use credit unless it's over $10. Cash only for this purchase."

I sighed. "I'm only five cents away, Arthur. I'm sorry I said the thing about the sprinkles. Please. Help me out?"

Wayne stepped forward, holding a ten-dollar bill. "Here, let me."

"You don't have to do that," I said. "I can buy another candy bar or something to put it over $10."

"I know I don't have to do it." Wayne smirked. "And I'm not doing it for free, either. I'm going to tax you one of those spicy tortilla chips."

Oh boy. Wayne was definitely flirting. Unless I was completely crazy. Also a distinct possibility.

I returned Wayne's smirk. "That sounds like a fair arrangement."

I picked up a bag of chips from the counter and gently pried the top part. The bag opened with a quiet pop.

Another look up at Wayne. He was looking at me, not at the chips.

I turned. Extended the bag of chips toward Wayne. He took a step toward me. Closer than he needed to be. The chips were the only thing between us. He didn't break eye contact as he reached into the bag and pulled out a chip. He kept looking at me as he slowwwlllyyy put the chip into his mouth.

I laughed and looked away. I noticed Arthur staring at us like, "what in the world is happening right now?"

"Good chip," Wayne said.

"I'm glad you like it," I said in my best sultry voice. "It's my favorite chip."

"Good to know," Wayne said. "But don't think this means we're friends again."

"Who said anything about friends?" I said. "We're just two people making a chip-for-cash exchange in a gas station."

"I'm off duty right now. That's all. So I can be Officer Friendly. But if I had my badge? If we were at the station? I would be obliged to remind you to stay out of my investigation into the Turtles' deaths. It's none of your beeswax."

"And I'd remind you that you're an idiot if you think KP could be a killer. And nobody says beeswax anymore."

"Good thing we're not at the station, then." Wayne reached out for another chip. I let him have it.

"So is one of you going to pay or not?" Arthur crossed his arms. His voice shattered the bizarre romantic moment Wayne and I had been sharing over spicy chips.

Wayne laughed and handed Arthur the cash. "Keep the change."

"Wow, the whole nickel?" Arthur sneered.

I gathered my snacks from the counter and headed toward the exit. I turned back to Wayne before I left. "Thanks for the snacks."

Wayne smiled. "Don't party too hard. At least, not without me."

When I got back into the car, Teeny and Miss May hooted and hollered like they had just seen a steamy deleted scene from *North Port Diaries.*

Teeny leaned forward. "That man was way closer than he needed to be to eat one of those chips! How did he smell? Was he a polite chewer? He looked good in those jeans!"

"Teeny! Leave her alone. She was just having a sensual chip-sharing experience in front of Arthur at the gas station. Not a big deal."

"It really wasn't a big deal," I said. "I don't know what you're talking about, even. I didn't have cash, so he paid."

Teeny and Miss May oohed and ahhhed even more at the revelation that Wayne had purchased the snacks for me.

"He paid! That makes it a date!" Teeny squealed.

Wayne walked past the pickup and gave me a little head nod. I thought Teeny and Miss May might explode with suppressed squeals and giggles.

"Is it me, or did it just get hot in here?" Teeny asked, fanning herself. "This is just like an episode of the *North Port Diaries* where the cute young girl falls for the hunky detective, but then he turns out to be a secret art thief, and he's not even American, he's from the Ukraine!"

"Wayne is not from the Ukraine," I said. "And this is not like that."

I handed the snacks back to Teeny, and she rifled through my collection. "What!? No sprinkles?"

I shook my head. "Nope. I gave Arthur an earful about it."

"Yelling at Arthur about sprinkles does more harm than good," Teeny said. "Trust me. I've learned from experience. In fact, I think he purposefully avoids sprinkled snacks just to spite me. Also, you never told me. How was Detective Hudson on the smell-o-meter?"

I shook my head and chunked the pickup into gear. *Wayne smelled great. Manly. Like cinnamon and leather.* But I didn't feel like talking about it.

The Turtles' Hamptons beach house was a two-story, blue-gray colonial with brown shingles and bright white trim. The place had more of an upscale cottage feel then the beachside-mansion-vibe that I'd expected. And I hated to admit it, but the place was tasteful and charming. The exact type of home I'd want to return to after a long day at the beach. Looking at it, I could see myself dragging a boogie board up to the foot of the steps, kicking off my sandals, rinsing off my feet and heading inside for a popsicle and a good book.

The front lawn was small but well-manicured, with a white picket fence. And the house seemed surprisingly homey. Quaint, even. Un-Turtle-like in every way. Maybe they hadn't been all bad.

"They must have really been hard up for cash," Miss May said.

"Why do you say that?" I asked. "I know this place is small but it's still the Hamptons. It would probably go for at least a million."

Miss May pointed across the lawn. "That's why."

A "For Sale" sign had been staked into the ground. I wasn't sure how I had missed it on my first appraisal of the house, but the sign looked fresh, like it hadn't been there more than a few weeks.

"I guess Reginald really did squander their savings on that fake land," I said. "Why would he even want property in the Netherlands?"

"But then why would the Germany brat kill them?" Teeny asked. "What's the point in killing your rich parents for their money if they lost all their money?"

"Good question," Miss May said. "We should ask him if he's home."

Miss May followed a mossy brick path to the front door and knocked. Teeny and I followed, hanging back one or two steps. We waited a few seconds, but no one answered.

"Why is it that every time we go to question a suspect, they never seem to be home?" I asked.

As if on cue, the front door opened. And there stood a sad-looking man. Late 60s. With a stringy ponytail, wearing a blazer with elbow patches. It took me a moment to place him, and then I remembered. The man was Linda Turtle's brother. He had been at Teeny's restaurant after Linda turned up dead.

"Can I help you?" The man had a sharp tone and did not seem to appreciate our arrival.

"Maybe," Miss May said. "But I don't know that we've officially met. Are you Linda's brother?"

"Dennis. Yes." The man narrowed his eyes. "You are?"

"My name is Mabel Thomas. My business partner KP has been arrested for Linda's murder."

Dennis stepped back. "What do you want?"

"I want to get KP out of jail. He's innocent. And I think you can help me prove that."

Dennis looked over his shoulder into the house then returned his gaze to Miss May. "I don't have time for that. I'm sorry." The man closed the door, but Miss May stopped it with her foot.

"I just need a few moments," Miss May said. "You may have information that can help free my associate."

Dennis checked his watch. "I don't have any helpful information. I can promise you that."

"Why are you in such a hurry, Dennis?" Miss May wedged the door open a bit and poked her head inside. Dennis stepped sideways to block her line of sight.

Teeny and I exchange a concerned look. *Was it possible that Dennis was the killer?* He was acting skittish, and his behavior gave me an uneasy feeling.

"I'm not in a hurry," Dennis said. "I just have to go somewhere."

"So you are in a hurry? You know you can use your phone to scan tickets for a plane these days, right?"

"I'm not getting on a plane," Dennis said.

"Then why do you have airline tickets in your pocket?" Miss May gestured towards Dennis's front pants pocket.

There, a small envelope protruded. Something was printed on the envelope in tiny text. I couldn't read it, and I doubted Miss May could either. I assumed she was making an educated guess.

"I have to go," Dennis said, tucking the envelope deeper into his pocket. "That is not a plane ticket."

"I think it is," Miss May said. "I think you're headed out of the country."

"That's preposterous!" Dennis's sudden indignation reminded me of his sister, and for the first time, I saw a striking family resemblance.

Miss May poked her head inside. "Is it? I notice your lamps are unplugged. I also notice you don't have any windows open. That's odd for a warm summer eve on the island, isn't it? Most people want that cross breeze. And I don't hear an air-conditioning unit either. All of that is strange enough, and I haven't even mentioned the large bag that you've been struggling to hide behind the door."

Dennis snorted. "I don't like cross breezes. How about that? Please leave."

Miss May didn't budge. "I'm not going to prevent you from going anywhere, Dennis. I just want you to answer one question."

Dennis sighed. "Fine. What?"

"Is Germany Turtle here?"

Dennis scrunched up his face. "Germany is in Africa studying for another eleven months. Did Linda not brag about that to you within moments of meeting you? I'm shocked."

Miss May shook her head. "No. Linda did boast quite freely about Germany's studies. But I thought, given the circumstances, he might have taken a hiatus. Are you sure he's not here? Have you heard from him?"

"As a matter of fact, I have." Dennis pulled his phone out of his pocket and opened up his emails. "Germany has too many demands on his time to send many emails from Africa. But he does manage to send a message at least once per week. His most recent correspondence arrived at 3 AM, just this morning."

Dennis flicked through a few emails then opened the message from Germany. He read part of the message aloud.

"'Dear family, here in Africa, things are well. The longer my stay here stretches on, the more I feel that I'm becoming one of the lions. I study them, and in that pursuit, I become one with the beasts. They are equal parts ballerina and wrecking ball. I wish to emulate their grace, poise, and primal aggression when I return stateside. That is all for now. The hotel accommodations are outstanding. I eat fresh fruit and world-class croissants for breakfast every morning. But my time with the lions keeps me grounded and has given me perspective for which I will be eternally grateful. Please see a photo of me eating breakfast. Attached.'"

Dennis opened the photo of Germany eating breakfast and held it out for us to see. There was a mid-20s man, blonde, with a sweater tied around his neck, eating a crois-sant. He was a Turtle down to his very marrow, to be sure. *He was also kinda cute*, I thought. *In a horrible, rich-kid- with-a-sweater-around-his-neck way.*

Dennis sniffled. "Isn't he the spitting image of Linda?"

It surprised me to see anyone so emotional about Linda. It surprised me even more that Germany Turtle had found someone to serve him fresh croissants in the wilds of Africa. I had assumed he was roughing it, out in the wilderness. *Stupid assumption.*

"The truth is, Germany doesn't know. Not about any of this. I haven't told him anything about his parents. I promised the police I would get in touch with Germany, but...I haven't been able to bring myself to break the tragic news."

Miss May rested a hand on Dennis's shoulder. "That makes sense. What could he do from so far away?"

Dennis nodded. "That's how I feel. Why ruin his trip for naught? Why not preserve Germany's innocence for just a few more weeks?"

"That croissant looked good," Teeny said. Miss May shot Teeny a look. "What? It seems like a delicious pastry. I can't say that?"

"The boy has exquisite taste, like his mother," Dennis said. "Now if you'll excuse me, you were correct. I'm off to a faraway land." Dennis grabbed a large suitcase from behind the door and stepped outside past Miss May. As if by magic, a hybrid sedan pulled up to the foot of the driveway and Dennis opened the rear passenger door.

Miss May watched him get in the car without so much as a single move to stop him.

"What are we doing?" I asked in a panicked whisper. "He was acting so guilty. Now he's getting away!"

"He wasn't acting guilty," Miss May said. "He was acting scared."

"Yeah," Teeny said. "Scared of getting caught!"

Miss May shook her head. "I don't think so. I think Dennis was afraid that whoever killed Linda and Reginald wants to kill him next."

"But we're never going to find him now," Teeny said. "What if you're wrong? With no Germany in the picture, Dennis was our only suspect."

"Lucky for us, we know where he's going." Miss May smiled.

I scratched my head. "How?"

"That envelope? It was from Jamaican Me Crazy Cruise Lines. Their branding is surprisingly subtle, but I recognized their logo."

I raised my eyebrows, impressed with Miss May's sleuthing. "Wow. That guy was so...I don't know, pale and stringy? He didn't strike me as a tropical cruise type."

"Everybody likes all-inclusive chicken fingers," Miss May said. "Especially when they're afraid of being murdered. Come on. Let's go around back."

23

BREAKING AND ENTERING, AGAIN

Out back, the small yard was in disarray. What had once been an elegant garden was overgrown. A rusted diving board hovered above a small in-ground pool with crumbling tile. A basketball hoop hung akimbo off an outbuilding, dangling as if it could fall at any moment.

The dilapidated space told a sad story of the once-great Turtles. Linda, Reginald, and Germany had been a family. They had jumped off that diving board and shot around on the basketball hoop. As time wore on, some dissent or resentment must have wormed its way into the family and rotted their relationships from the inside out. At least that's what seemed to have happened between Linda and Reginald.

Like the love between the Turtles, this untended yard had decayed into an ugly shadow of its former self. *I guess sometimes that's what happens when we're not looking. If you ignore a garden, it dies. Just like the Turtles.* But someone had killed the Turtles. And we still weren't any closer to knowing who.

Miss May tried the back door and the windows, but everything was locked.

Teeny grabbed a hunk of crumbling stone from near the pool. "Let's bash our way in!"

"Don't you think that might draw the attention of the neighbors?" Miss May asked.

Teeny shrugged. "I'll bash gently."

"Are you two sure we shouldn't follow Dennis or something?" I asked. "He was trying to leave from the moment we arrived. It was pretty fishy."

Miss May jostled another window. "I don't think Dennis wanted to talk to us, you're right about that. But it doesn't mean he killed his sister."

"He just had a murderous vibe," I insisted. "Like, he looked exactly like a mugshot of a murderer."

Miss May turned back to me. "You can't judge a murderer by their hypothetical mugshot. It just doesn't feel right to me. It's not like Linda and Dennis were having a secret affair. They were brother and sister."

"Then maybe it was about money," Teeny said. "Or maybe they weren't actually related! Maybe he was adopted from the Ukraine and—"

"No one is from the Ukraine, Teeny," Miss May said.

Teeny threw up her hands. "Okay. Don't come crawling back to me when the killer turns out to be Ukrainian."

"I don't think it was about money, either," Miss May said. "The Turtles bought Petunia's house because it was in foreclosure. And they're trying to sell this place. Anyone close to them surely knew there wasn't much of an inheritance to be had."

"Other than the life insurance policy that Reginald cashed in on," I said.

"And that's why we're looking for Germany," Miss May

said. "He would be entitled to that money in the event of Reginald's death."

"Excuse me?" A tiny old lady approached from the next yard over. She was no more than 4'10" tall, and she was wearing a giant straw hat to keep out the sun. It blocked the entire top half of her face. Her voice was high and brittle.

"Who are you people? I have pepper spray, and I'm not afraid to use it! My grandson made it from actual hot peppers he grew in his garden. He says it would blind a full-grown man. He's an odd boy but very good. Very smart and capable with his hands. Loves science."

I held in a laugh. The more threatening she tried to seem, the more innocuous she became.

"Don't laugh at me," she trilled. "I will pepper you up!"

Miss May stepped toward the elderly neighbor. "No need to pepper anyone up. We're just here trying to check into our BnB. We booked this place online, and the man who lives here, Dennis Turtle? He told us the key would be in a lockbox out back but we can't find it. I am going to leave him the worst review. We drove here all the way from the city for a weekend by the beach. I'm exhausted. I need to use the bathroom!"

"Oh." The old lady put her homemade pepper spray away. "You have a reservation to stay here through some sort of bed-and-breakfast online?"

Miss May nodded and repeated some crucial information. "Dennis Turtle rented the home to us. Chelsea, show this kind woman the reservation."

Uh, right. It just has to exist first.

I opened my phone and quickly typed out a reservation in my notepad. TURTLE HOUSE RESERVATION, PARTY OF 3. KEY IN LOCK BOX OUT BACK.

I stepped forward and showed the old woman the note.

"He emailed this out earlier." I shot a look at Miss May. *Thanks for putting me on the spot.* "We just can't seem to find the key."

The old woman nodded. "That looks like an official receipt. Thank you. Now you say you need the key?"

"That's right," Miss May said.

"I know where the key is. I'm queen of the neighborhood watch. Everyone tells me where their spare keys are. The Turtles, well, they're unique. It's not just under the mat. It's more, uh, thematically appropriate than that."

The woman gestured at a dozen ceramic turtles resting near the back door. "Care to guess which turtle will show you inside?"

Miss May laughed. "That sounds fun. But very confusing for a BnB guest."

The old woman smiled as Miss May squatted down to get a good look at each turtle. There was a pink turtle, and a blue turtle. There was a longneck turtle and even a snapping turtle. At last, Miss May selected the center turtle and looked under its belly.

Turtle behold. There was the key!

The ancient neighbor smiled. "How did you know?"

Miss May shrugged. "You were looking right at it."

"Well," the woman said. "I never did have much of a poker face. Let me know if you need any recommendations for our neighborhood. It's a beautiful place."

We thanked the old woman and opened the door to the house.

Miss May ran her finger along a windowsill and turned back to us. "There are clues in this home. They will be obvious to anyone perceptive enough to spot them. We just have to look in the right places."

I glanced around. The place was well-decorated with eclectic, rustic furniture. Like each piece was the artisan-crafted, rustic version of something that might be sold at a department store. The house was spotless. Not a stitch of clutter or a speck of dirt. Spic and span and utterly clueless.

"I suppose the fact that the house is so clean could be a clue," I said.

Miss May tapped her nose. "Not exactly what I was thinking, but I like that. Go on."

"OK. You don't think the cleanliness is a clue? Then maybe it has something to do with this nice furniture. I assumed this place would be empty."

"Tell me more," Miss May prodded.

"Well, if the Turtles went as broke on that Netherlands deal as they claimed, wouldn't they have sold off their nice pieces? Or at the very least, moved all this stuff to Pine Grove so they wouldn't have to pay to furnish Petunia's?"

"Logical assumption," Miss May said. "And a keen observation. But I'm afraid your wrongness hangs heavy in the air."

I groaned. Miss May was settling a little too comfortably into her role as famed local detective. I wanted my own sleuthing skills to be up to snuff. And cat and mouse games are less fun when you're the mouse. While I had nothing against mice, I'd always thought of myself as a more exotic rodent, like a capybara. *But I digress.*

"Don't groan, Chelsea," Miss May said. "You're getting there. Teeny, what do you think?"

"My theory involves the Ukraine," Teeny said. "I prefer to keep it to myself."

"Wait!" I crouched down to get a better look at the couch. Then I scuttled over to the coffee table and looked beneath. I jumped to my feet with a triumphant pump of my fist. "I figured it out!"

I took an enthusiastic step toward Miss May, tripped on the expensive rug, and fell sideways onto the ground. "This isn't their furniture!" I yelled as I went down.

Teeny and Miss May helped me to my feet.

"What do you mean this isn't their furniture?" Teeny asked. "It's in their house. Do you think it belongs to the creepy Jamaican cruiser?"

"All the furniture is brand new," I said. "The tags are still on the bottom. I don't know how I missed it. This house has been staged! I've done this exact thing a thousand times. You go into someone's home when it's for sale, and you place exquisite furniture as though someone still lives there. It helps people imagine themselves in the space."

"I don't know," Teeny said. "Maybe the Turtles just had new stuff. They were snobby like that. I could see them throwing all their furniture out every six months."

"I thought that," I said. "But there's no TV in the living room. Look."

Teeny looked around the room. She spun in a circle. She got on her hands and knees and looked under the table. "You're right. Who doesn't have a TV these days? That creeps me out."

"It's not that weird in a staged house, though. Actually, eliminating the TV is a staging technique straight out of the books. You frame the furniture around a focal point that's not the TV, like a fireplace. Even though people are obsessed with TV in real life, it never looks right in these old houses where the mantle is the natural focal point."

Miss May clapped her hands. She smiled. "Well done, Chelsea. This home is staged for sale. Even I didn't notice that right away. Sadly, the staged furniture is not the clue I was searching for."

"What? What do you mean? You said there were obvious clues. What's more obvious than that?"

"You were getting pretty warm when you mentioned the fireplace."

I looked at the fireplace, then back to Miss May. "I was?"

She nodded. "Dennis Turtle had a fire going earlier today. Can't you smell it?"

Teeny and I sniffed the air.

"I guess I have been smelling something smoky," Teeny said. "I thought it was some kind of fancy fire-scented air freshener."

"I didn't notice it at all," I said. "I got too caught up in the furniture."

Miss May grinned. "Odd to light a fire on a warm day like today, isn't it?"

I crossed to the fireplace, squatted down, and took a look. "You want to know what's even odder?" I turned back to Miss May. "All the ashes have been cleaned away."

I held my hand above the grill. "But it's still warm. You're right. Dennis had a fire going. Recently."

"He was burning something," Teeny said. "But what?"

24

ASHES TO ASHES

Three large black trash cans lined the side of the house. Teeny whistled in appreciation as we approached.

"Those are some classy trash cans," she said. "And look at how sturdy they are."

Teeny patted one of the trash receptacles as if it were a big dog. "You're a good trashcan, aren't you? You hold up in bad weather. You keep raccoons out. Yes, you do."

"Teeny?" Miss May stepped toward the trash. "We're hunting for evidence here. Not trying to decide which trashcan we want to bring home from the pound."

Teeny jutted out her lower lip. "You're no fun." She stepped aside, and Miss May opened the lid of the first trash can.

I stood on my tippy-toes to get a look over Miss May's shoulder into the can. Sure enough, there was a single white trash bag at the bottom of the bin. And the whole container smelled like ash. Miss May reached into the can and pulled out the bag.

"Taking the trash out already?" The old lady neighbor peered over her fence from the adjacent yard.

Thunk. Miss May dropped the bag back into the can and smiled. "That's right!"

"How do you generate that much garbage in such a short period of time?" The old woman narrowed her eyes. Maybe she was a sleuth in her own right.

"Oh, well..." Miss May hesitated for a moment, and I couldn't take the tension.

"We brought the garbage from home," I said with an odd amount of enthusiasm. "Why dirty up your own trash can when you're paying for access to someone else's?"

The old woman shook her head. "This is exactly why I don't rent my home while I'm away. People are so weird."

Miss May shot me a look and smiled at the nosy neighbor. "People certainly are weird. Some people just do and say the craziest things. When they don't need to do or say anything."

I shrugged. *I did my best!*

"Whatever," the woman said. Then she ducked back behind her fence, muttering to herself about strangers and garbage cans and the state of the world.

I watched through a crack in the fence until the old woman disappeared back inside her home. Then I turned back to Miss May and gave a thumbs-up.

Miss May gingerly lifted the bag out of the trash and padded back inside. I followed close behind, but Teeny hung back.

"Teeny," I whispered. "Are you coming?"

"Yeah," Teeny said. "This is just the nicest trash can I've ever seen. I'd like to order some for Grandma's. Maybe in blue."

I held the door open and motioned Teeny inside. "I'll

look online. But come on. Don't you want to see what's in that bag?"

Once we were safely back inside the Turtles' Hamptons getaway, Miss May rushed to the kitchen table and opened the trash bag. She was about to dump the contents of the bag onto the table when I reached out to stop her.

"Wait!" I cried out. "This is an expensive table. Don't get ash all over it."

"Lives are on the line, Chelsea," Miss May said impatiently.

"Give me one second," I said, scanning the room. "I'll put something down on the table."

I understood the urgency of the situation, but I also appreciated the beautiful table and wanted to protect it. The house was staged so well, there were no loose odds or ends to cover the table. Not even a spare piece of fabric. So I unbuttoned my shirt and flung it across the table.

"Whoa-ho, getting a little PG-13 in here!" Teeny said. Then she cracked up laughing. "Hang on a second. Do you have slices of pizza on your bra?"

I looked down. *Teeny was not wrong.* I picked the wrong day to wear my cartoon pizza bra.

"Don't get distracted!" I said. "Let's see what's in the bag."

Teeny doubled over with laughter. Miss May chuckled too.

"That is ridiculous," Miss May said. "Let me guess. Your undies have little pictures of cookies on them."

I cringed.

"Wait! Am I right?" Miss May's eyes widened as she waited for my answer.

I looked down. "My undies also have pizza on them."

Teeny and Miss May both cracked up.

"You guys," I protested. "My undergarments are not what's important right now. Who cares if they're pizza-themed? They're comfortable!"

Neither Teeny nor Ms. May seemed capable of getting a grip, so I grabbed the trash bag and dumped the contents onto my shirt.

Much of the bag had been reduced to ash. But among the ashes were several pieces of charred paper. I picked up a scrap.

"This is a newspaper article." I held out the paper to Miss May. "Looks like part of a headline. See?"

Miss May took the scrap and squinted at it. "The only word I can make out is 'robbery.'"

Teeny ran her fingers through the pile of ashes. "There are more scraps of paper here. Maybe we can figure the rest out?"

I grabbed another scrap from the pile. "Here's the date. July 19. Ten years ago."

"Here's something else," I said and extracted another fragment. The paper was singed around the edges but I could make out one important detail. "The robber made out with over $3 million."

Teeny gasped. "Here's another shred of paper! The Yankees lost by three in extra innings. Oh. Maybe that's less relevant."

"Maybe we should piece this all together like a puzzle and see what we get," Miss May suggested.

I nodded and silently slid a few pieces into place. Teeny and Miss May stepped back as I worked. I was usually quick at puzzles so they let me do my thing. Most of the article had been reduced to nothing, but after several minutes I had compiled snippets of a few sentences or phrases for us to read.

"...murderous intruder." "...threatened customers." "...armed and dangerous."

I was about to give up when I found one last intriguing snippet. I read it aloud, "'The photo above shows a police sketch of the criminal.'"

"I don't understand," Miss May said. "This person robbed the bank without even a mask on? Do we have any pieces of the sketch?"

I sifted through the ash on the table. "There's a few more scraps of paper. Let me see what I can put together."

"Do you think Dennis was the burglar?" Teeny asked.

Miss May shook her head. "I don't know. I suppose it's possible. Or maybe Linda or Reginald robbed the bank, and Dennis knew about it?"

"They didn't seem like bank robbers to me," Teeny said. "But then again, they were snobs who lost their fortune. Desperate times."

I held up a piece of paper. "I think I found a nose!"

Teeny peered over my shoulder. "Oh yeah. That's a schnoz. Do you think the police can identify someone based on their schnoz?"

"I doubt it," Miss May said. "Although it seems clear that whoever this burglar was, he or she escaped that day without being caught. And probably this robber person has something to do with Linda and Reginald's death."

My phone rang. I took a subtle look under the table. *Mike. Forwarding that to voicemail, thank you very much.* Thank goodness Teeny and Miss May didn't catch that one. I'd never live it down.

I turned my attention back to the pile of ashes, hoping to find an eye or maybe an ear, but then someone knocked on the front door.

A feeble voice called out. "Hello? I know you're not here for a bed and breakfast!"

Teeny, Miss May and I exchanged worried glances. "It's the neighbor lady," I said. "What are we going to do?"

Miss May shrugged and Teeny called out, "We're busy. Come back later! We didn't order any pizza."

"We have plenty of pizza on our panties," Miss May added quietly. I glared.

"I have the spare-spare key," the woman shouted back. "I only rang the bell as a polite warning. I'm coming in."

A key turned in the door. I took a step back.

More of that nosy neighbor was the last thing our investigation needed.

"I'm just off the phone with Dennis! He says this home is not being rented." The woman walked toward our pile of ashes with outsized authority.

"There must be a mistake," Miss May said.

"No mistake," the woman croaked. "Dennis said with absolute certainty. 'No guests allowed.' So what are you doing here? What's on the table? Is this girl wearing a pizza brassiere?"

"This is just a puzzle," I said. "We're playing a game. On vacation. As people do."

"Who breaks into someone's house, pretending they're staying at a BnB, and plays a game?"

Teeny stepped forward. "We didn't break in. You let us in! Showed us the key, ya old bag!"

Miss May held Teeny back with one arm. "What my friend means is…" Miss May searched for an out. "Dennis must be mistaken. We rented this home from Linda and Reginald Turtle. I can give them a call if you'd like."

The old woman huffed and puffed. "You most certainly cannot! Those Turtles are dead!"

I found a scrap of paper with what appeared to be a sketch of a mouth on it and lined it up beneath the nose, slowly forming a portrait of the burglar. "I got a mouth!"

The woman pushed her way toward me. "What now? What are you talking about? Is this the trash you were digging around in earlier?"

"No. It's nothing. Never mind!"

I turned away from the woman and kept hunting through the ashes. I found a cheek, then another ear, then part of what might have been a forehead. A face began to form.

"This is not a regular puzzle," the woman said. "This is stolen trash! Taking someone else's garbage is a felony. I'm sure of it."

"Nu-uh," Teeny said. "That's stolen mail you're thinking of. Trash is up for grabs. One man's trash is another man's puzzle! This BnB has subpar entertainment. There's no TV! We had to get creative."

The woman placed her hands on her hips. "One man's trash is that man's trash for the entire time it's on his property."

I took cover behind Teeny and stepped back to look at my work. I had a few features, but the face was no more recognizable than a Mr. Potato Head. Teeny and the old neighbor woman were about to come to blows over the legality of stealing trash, so I stepped between them.

"Teeny! It's OK. The puzzle is missing pieces. Forget it."

Teeny turned to me. "Are you sure?"

I nodded. "Also, I think I may have taken us to the wrong address." I turned to the angry woman. "We were looking for the Turtles' East Hampton property. Is this the wrong part of the island?"

The woman clutched her chest as though I had just hurled a fat loogie of an insult. "This is South Hampton! East Hampton is far less upscale."

"That explains it." I shot a glance at Miss May. "Sorry. I took us to the wrong Turtle house."

"I wasn't even aware the Turtles had a home in that ghetto," the woman said.

"They're ashamed of it," I said. "I'm sure."

"That makes sense," the woman said. "Well. I'm glad that's settled. Time for you all to go then?"

I nodded. "Time for us to go."

25

POTHOLES IN PARADISE

B y the time we got out to the pickup and lurched onto the main road, Miss May's sleuth-brain had already kicked into high gear.

"Where can we access those old newspaper articles? Someone has to have a copy still intact," she said. "Should we try the local library?"

"I don't think the library is a good idea," I said. Then I pointed at the building across the street, an old library with a sign out front that read "Library Closed Due to Lack of Funding. Thanks for Nothing."

"Ha!" Teeny laughed. "I mean, awww. That's sad for that library. But I like their sign. It's sassy."

"I agree," Miss May said. "Clever signage. But if that local library isn't open anymore... Do we have any hope of finding a copy of those articles?"

"It's possible that the library digitized the papers before it closed," I said. "But we would need access to some sort of special educational or journalistic databases for that."

"How do you know?" Teeny asked.

I shrugged. "I worked on some restoration projects in

Manhattan a couple years ago. The furniture needed to be accurate to the era. I had to get authorization from NYU to use their libraries. Even then, I needed a grad student to help me navigate the databases."

"Your job is so cool," Teeny said. "I want to be an interior designer."

"It was cool," I said, emphasizing was. "Too bad Mike stole all my clients, and I had to crawl back to Pine Grove with my tail all chewed up."

Teeny leaned forward. "Was that Mike who called you in there?"

"Who else would be calling her?" Miss May said.

I guess they noticed.

"Maybe that detective with the keg for a chest and tree trunks for legs," Teeny said.

"That is not an attractive description," I said.

"How would you describe his chest?" Miss May asked.

"I wouldn't!" I said. "Can we get back to the investigation please?"

"Right! The databases," Miss May said. "I have an idea."

Miss May pulled out her phone, made a call and put it on speaker. Two rings later, a female voice answered.

"This is Liz. Editor-In-Chief, Pine Grove Gazette. Everything you say is on the record unless you request otherwise."

"Liz. It's May. I want this off the record."

"One second. I'll turn the recorder off." A second passed. Liz returned to the line. "OK. It's off."

"You record all conversations unless someone asks you not to?" Miss May asked.

"I'm a reporter," Liz said. "What do you need?"

Miss May shook her head. "I need access to some databases. We're looking for an old newspaper article from a Hamptons publication."

"Too time-consuming. I'm working a big story right now. New pothole on Commerce Street. It's scandalous. Not enough hours in the day. Sorry."

"This is bigger than a pothole," Miss May said.

"The pothole is two feet wide and two feet deep."

"Two feet deep?! That's a regular hole," I said. "Not a pothole."

"Is Chelsea there?" Liz asked. "I appreciate being informed when I'm on speaker. I'd do the same for you."

"Always assume Chelsea is with me," Miss May said.

"I'm here too, Liz," Teeny said. "How's your mother?"

"She's well."

"And your brother and sisters?" Teeny asked.

"Also well," Liz said. "I'll tell them you said hi."

Miss May covered the phone. "Can you stop with the small talk, Teeny?"

Teeny winced. "Sorry."

Miss May uncovered the phone. "So. Liz. I respect your pothole."

"Or regular-sized hole," Liz said. "I like that angle."

"Right. I respect the hole," Miss May continued. "But I promise this story is bigger. And I'll give you the scoop after we solve it. But only if you help us."

"I can work any story I want," Liz said.

"But only one person will have exclusive access to the team that solved the Turtle murders. And I'm not above going to the Hudson Valley News with this intel."

There was a long silence on the other end of the line. Liz yelled at someone to stay away from her pothole. We heard steps crunching over gravel. Then the sound of Liz getting in her car and slamming the door behind her.

"OK," Liz said. "This better be good."

The next morning, Miss May and I headed to the library to meet Liz. We stopped at Grandma's to pick up Teeny on our way, but the restaurant had a line out the door. People had heard great things about Petey's cuisine, and they were ready to pay big bucks for his cooking. Apparently his stick food wasn't too fancy after all. It was like the Hashbrown Lasagna craze all over again.

Teeny had spent so long encouraging Petey to do something productive with his life, she took his success as a success of her own. She had decided to work as a waitress to support Petey's big day, and she didn't complain at all when we told her we'd have to meet up with Liz on our own. OK, she actually complained a lot, but she got over it. I made a mental note to pop back for more of Petey's fries later, then Miss May and I left, on a mission. As usual.

When Miss May and I entered the library, Liz was knee-deep in an argument with a surly, bearded librarian. Liz was red-faced and angry, while the librarian appeared bored and on the edge of sleep.

"I cannot believe this," Liz said. "I demand to speak to your manager."

"I don't have a manager," the bearded man said. "I'm a volunteer."

Miss May approached with a gentle smile. "Is there a problem, Liz?"

"There is a problem, as a matter of fact. Ask this sleepy librarian. He'll tell you all about it."

The sleepy librarian shrugged. "The main library is flooded. Only computers available are in the children's area."

"That should be okay," Miss May said. "We can go in there."

"When's the last time you worked in the children's library?" Liz asked.

Miss May shrugged. "I can't remember. Maybe never?"

"Well," Liz said. "You're in for a treat."

To be honest, when I found out that we would be working in the children's library, I was excited. I loved children's libraries. They were always so bright and fun and alive. A stark contrast to the beige, bland grown-up libraries that are so often found in small towns.

But when we entered the children's area, I understood what Liz had meant. There was only one computer. It was about two feet off the ground. And the only chairs for the computer were tiny little beanbags that looked like cupcakes. Not exactly a perch befitting a future Pulitzer prize-winning journalist.

"This is ridiculous," Liz said. "That computer is tiny. And look! It's connected to a construction paper drawing of a tree? Absurd."

I followed Liz's gaze up from the computer. Indeed, a tree had been papier-mâchéd on the wall above the machine. The computer looked like a knot in the big paper oak tree, and there was even a plastic owl drawn above the monitor. *Plastic*, I thought, remembering Salazar's words. *Everything is plastic.* I shuddered at the memory, but it didn't seem particularly pertinent at the moment.

"I promise this will be worth sitting on the cupcake chair," Miss May said. "If we find the information we need you could be helping us solve one of the biggest cases in the history of this town."

Liz raised her eyebrows. "Really? You said this was

bigger than the pothole, but you never said it could be so monumental."

Miss May turned on the computer, and it booted up. "We won't know just how big it is unless you can get me into those databases."

Liz smiled. "Give me 30 seconds, and I'll have all the information you need."

Two hours later, Liz had located the appropriate database and gained access to the Hamptons Tribune, which was the publication we needed.

"You said you had a date?" Liz asked. I handed Liz a slip of paper with the date printed on it. "Good thing. We'd be hopeless without this."

I smiled. Liz didn't dish out compliments with much frequency, so it felt extra-validating to be on her good side. A few clicks of the mouse later, and Liz had accessed every article written during the month in question. She muttered as she scrolled through the articles. "July 19... Robbery... Three million..." Then she perked up. "Got it!"

Liz clicked on the article and a story filled the screen, its headline familiar from the pile of scraps and ashes. The words popped up quickly, but the sketch of the burglar loaded with excruciating slowness.

"Where's the photo?" Miss May asked.

Liz pointed at an empty box inlaid on the article. "It's loading. These old servers take forever with images sometimes. Do you guys want to read the article while we wait? Or I could read it to you?"

Miss May chuckled. "Would you like to read the article to us, Liz?"

Liz smiled. "It would be good training for my future as an on-camera personality."

"Alright," Miss May said. "Go ahead."

26

THE BIG REVEAL

L iz cleared her throat and began to read.

"Police are investigating after a bank was robbed on Wednesday afternoon by a woman wearing a mask of a United States president who shall not be named."

"Why won't they name the President?" Miss May asked. "Who cares?"

"Yeah," I said. "That's weird."

"Bad journalism," Liz said. "They should have described the mask in abundant detail. Details are the cornerstone of all good stories. Journalism is all about integrity and honesty and transparency, and when—"

"OK," Miss May said. "Please. Go on."

"K," Liz said. "No more interruptions."

"Sorry," Miss May said. "Continue."

Liz cleared her throat, shook out her arms to get loose, and kept reading.

"'According to authorities, the incident happened at the South Hampton Bank on the 400 block of Main Street just before 1 PM. Officials say, in addition to demanding money, the suspect threatened one of the tellers and several customers within the bank.' This copy is terrible."

"No editing on the go," Miss May said.

"Fine. Just...let it be known. I would have done a better job than this."

"Of course," Miss May said.

Liz continued. "'A security guard managed to unmask the burglar as the burglar made her escape. The police are now seeking a woman who resembles the composite sketch featured here.' That's referring to the photo we haven't seen."

Liz looked up from the article. The photo had loaded about five percent. We could see the top of a woman's head and what looked like a ponytail, but nothing more. Liz returned to the article.

"This article is way too long. My mouth is getting dry," Liz said.

"Do you want me to get you some water?" I asked.

"I'm fine," Liz said. "It's almost over."

She cleared her throat and kept reading. "The criminal is suspected of several additional crimes in Long Island and Queens over the past several years. These crimes include carjacking, mugging, and several other bank robberies. Notably, this so-called presidential criminal is also suspected of stealing several hot dog carts from a New York City hot dog cart supplier earlier this year.' That seems irrelevant."

"Who steals hot dog carts?" I asked.

"A burglar who likes hot dogs, I guess," Miss May said. Liz glared at us. We stopped talking, and she continued reading.

"Although no weapon was used in the heist, officials say the suspect kept motioning to her waist and yelling that she had a gun. No serious injuries were reported, although bank customer... Whoa, this is big! ...bank customer Linda Turtle complained that she twisted her ankle while attempting to flee.'"

I gasped and almost fell off my cupcake beanbag. "Linda Turtle! Linda Turtle was there when the bank was robbed."

Miss May leaned in to get a better look at the article. "Keep reading. Does it mention Reginald?"

Liz scanned the end of the article. "The suspect took off on foot, yada yada...got on a waiting motorcycle less than a block away and escaped going the wrong way on Baptist Church Road."

Liz scrolled to find more details from the article, but that's where it ended. "That's all they wrote," she said. "I can't believe this criminal was a woman."

"We're capable of robbing banks too, Elizabeth," Miss May said.

"I know," Liz said. "I'm a feminist, May. But stealing hot dog carts? That's gross."

I chuckled. Then I glanced back at the screen.

"The picture is almost loaded," I said. "Look!"

The photo was about halfway visible. We could see a face from the nose up. A woman's face, and she looked vaguely reminiscent of someone I knew...

"Who is that?" I asked. "I recognize those eyes."

The photo loaded another five percent and Miss May actually fell off her beanbag.

"Oh my goodness, Miss May said. "I know that woman... I know her well."

27

A CLEAN GETAWAY

Noreen lit up as we entered the dry-cleaner.

I tried to smile back, but it was hard, knowing she had robbed that bank.

And maybe killed the Turtles.

I still wanted to know what she had done, exactly.

And why she had done it.

And I was confident Miss May would get some answers.

But Noreen seemed so innocent as we approached. And I started to think maybe we were wrong. Maybe it was just like an episode of *North Port Diaries*, and Noreen had an evil twin who had robbed the banks and stolen the hot dog carts.

But the sketch in the paper looked so much like her.

Still, it had been ten years. Maybe Noreen didn't look the same? Maybe Miss May was wrong. Either way, I was about to find out.

"You two here for dry cleaning or just to chat?" Noreen said.

Miss May smiled. "Oh, we were over at Teeny's, just figured we'd pop in."

"I love it," Noreen said. "Pleasant encounters with people you love are the secret to small town happiness! You can help me decide. Is mid-September too soon for Halloween decorations?"

I tried to engage in the cover of small talk. "I say it's never too early."

"And I say wait another week," Miss May said.

Noreen chortled. "I'll split the difference and wait another three days."

Sure, I thought. *Unless you're in jail by then. Ya sleaze!*

"What else is new?" Noreen asked. "Can I get you girls coffee or something?"

She walked out from behind the counter and toward a little coffee station near the entrance. There were mints, and cookies, and even a popcorn machine for customers to use. Noreen poured herself a cup and lined up two others. "I just brewed a fresh pot."

"A fresh cup of coffee sounds good to me," I said, hoping to buy some time to poke around the shop. I nudged Miss May. "Would you like a cup?"

Miss May took my not-so-subtle hint. "Sure," she said. "Three sugars, two creams and a little honey if you have it."

"Honey. That sounds amazing," Noreen said. "I have some here for tea, so it's no problem at all."

Noreen got to work on the coffee, and I glanced around. The shop was simple. Bare bones, even. It did not look like the kind of business a bank robber would run. *Maybe that's because a bank robber wouldn't run any business,* I thought. *They would run. Literally. Out of the country!*

I turned back to Noreen. She hummed a happy song as she poured the coffee. I questioned our suspicions again. Noreen seemed so nice. But then the dry-cleaner turned back around, and her face had shifted.

"You're not just here for small talk are you, May?" Noreen asked.

Miss May put her hands in her pockets. "What makes you say that?"

"I don't know. You've never popped in on me before. And your energy feels off. You're looking at me like I robbed a bank or something."

"Interesting choice of words," I said. Then I clapped my hands over my mouth. *Why did I always talk at the exact wrong moments?*

"What did you say?" Noreen asked.

I shook my head. "Nothing. Just talking to myself. About cheese."

Noreen looked at Miss May. Miss May shrugged. "The girl loves cheese."

"Not moldy cheese though," I said. "I like the stuff with chemicals in it. American mostly. Although mozzarella is nice. If it's made fresh in one of the shops around here. You go to other parts of the country and the mozzarella is crud. Trust me. Don't ever eat mozzarella in the Midwest. Or the South, for that matter. Now cheddar in the Midwest? That's a different story. Wisconsin cheddar, straight out of those Wisconsin heifers, that stuff is—"

Mercifully, Miss May cut me off. "You know, Chels, you really shouldn't eat the stuff with chemicals. It's not good for you." My aunt turned to Noreen. "You ever worry about that in your business, Noreen?"

"The chemicals in cheese?"

"No," Miss May said. "The dry-cleaning chemicals. I've heard a lot of cleaners actually use <u>arsenic</u>."

Noreen turned and studied Miss May. Miss May stood strong, but I felt like I might pee in my pizza panties.

"I see what this is," Noreen said.

"Tell us then." Miss May said. "What is this?"

"You think you solved another mystery." Noreen sipped her coffee with a loud slurp. "But it pains me to tell you. This time, May? You haven't solved anything."

Miss May shook her head. "It pains me to tell you, Noreen. You're wrong."

Noreen returned to the coffee station. Added more cream to her cup.

"Here's how I see it," Miss May said. "You robbed a bank in the Hamptons. July. Ten years ago. It was the last robbery in a long string of crimes you committed. Including, for some reason, the theft of several hot dog carts while wearing the mask of an unspecified President. That bank robbery was the final and most tumultuous of your offenses. A security guard unmasked you. Customers in the bank saw your face. So you were forced into hiding. You traveled the world for the first few years to stay off the radar, a habit you maintain to this day. But you tired of life abroad so you moved to a quiet little town in upstate New York. To start again. And that worked well until the Turtles came to town. And Linda Turtle spotted you. And remembered you. And wanted to turn you in."

Noreen didn't turn back from the coffee bar. She stayed statue-still and listened.

All was quiet until I opened my big, stupid mouth again. "Wait, but the statute of limitations on robbing a bank has to be less than 10 years. Linda Turtle couldn't have turned Noreen in."

"Your niece makes an excellent point," Noreen said, back still turned to us.

"Of course," Miss May said. "Thank you, Chelsea. It makes even more sense this way. Linda didn't want to turn you in, did she? That would have been pointless, and what would she have had to gain? Justice was hardly a suitable motive for a woman like Linda Turtle. No...Linda wanted the money you stole. For her dream retirement in Milan."

Noreen laughed. "That's some tale, May. And I'm sorry to disappoint you. But I'm just a local dry-cleaner. That reality may not fit into your vision of the world, where everyone is a criminal, everyone a suspect. But I would never rob a bank. Nor would I kill Linda Turtle. Or her husband. Murder doesn't quite jive with my Eastern philosophy. I'm surprised at you, May. I've been nothing but kind to you."

"I know," Miss May said. "Strangely enough, your kindness will be your undoing."

Hmm. Cryptic. I listened closer.

"You didn't need to kill Reginald, but you got paranoid that prying eyes would turn to you, especially when you noticed we were working so hard to free the first person you tried to frame — KP. It was a smart idea, I guess, staging Reginald's suicide. But you left proof of your involvement behind."

Noreen scoffed. Miss May turned to me. "Chels, can I borrow your phone?"

I handed Miss May my phone, and she scrolled to the photo of Reginald's suicide note. She put the phone down beside Noreen. "See the note Reginald left? Look at the way he crosses his T's. Very low. And the D. The way he writes it, it's barely visible. I've never seen anyone with handwriting like that."

Miss May reached into her purse and pulled out the book Noreen had brought her from India. "Other than you."

Miss May opened the book to the note Noreen had written. Sure enough, all Noreen's D's and 'T's were as Miss May described. Noreen didn't even look at the proof in front of her.

"So now the amateur detective has turned into a handwriting expert?" Noreen asked.

"Well, it's not just the handwriting that looked odd to me," Miss May said. "It was also the fact that Reginald Turtle misspelled his only son's name. Unlikely, isn't it, that Reginald would write 'German' instead of 'Germany' in his own suicide note?"

For the first time, Noreen paled slightly. She recovered quickly and said with a smirk, "Seems to me you're getting rusty, May. There's no way I could've killed Reginald Turtle. I was at a church fundraiser that night." Noreen pointed at the coffee maker. "I won that coffee maker. Half the town was there. Feel free to ask around. Or taste the coffee. Both proof enough. Are you sure I can't get you a cup? Or are you so embarrassed you'd like to leave?"

"I'm not embarrassed," Miss May said. "I'm just getting started."

"Do you believe the alibi?" I whispered.

Miss May nodded. "I do believe the alibi. And that's what has led me to my new theory."

Noreen laughed. "I told you, May. I wasn't anywhere near that man when he died."

"I know you weren't," Miss May said. "But that's only because you instructed someone else to do the killing for you."

"Who?" I asked.

"The getaway driver."

28

THE PLOT GETS CHUNKY

"Everybody put your hands where I can see them!"

Dennis Turtle exploded toward us from the back of the shop, pointing a gun straight at Noreen. Noreen's jaw dropped when she saw him. "Dennis! What are you doing here? You idiot!"

"I am not an idiot!" Dennis' face reddened. "I am good enough. And smart enough. Just as good as any other Turtle!"

"The other Turtles are dead," Noreen said. "Now put the gun down, Dennis. You look foolish."

"I am not a fool!" Dennis took a step toward Noreen. "I may have been once. But getaway drivers deserve more than a 10% cut. And they deserve love. And to be treated well. Not forced to do the dirty work as you go gallivanting across the globe and run your cute little business in your cute little town. Do you know how hard it has been to stretch that 10%? I'm the laughing stock of my family!" Dennis's voice caught in his throat. "At least I was. Before you made me kill them off. But your threats mean nothing now. I demand my fair share of the money. I don't want to have to steal any more hot dog carts just to make a quick buck! I hated that mask and the hot dog juice burned my hands every single time!" *Well, that explains that, I guess.*

Dennis removed the safety on the gun and took another step toward Noreen. "Give me the money, Noreen. Now."

"There's nothing left, Dennis. Why do you think I opened this store? For my health?"

Dennis's hands shook. His nostrils flared. "You're lying! You're always lying. Why can't you respect me? Why can't you treat me fair?"

Dennis was, to put it bluntly, freaking the heck out. He was shaking and panting, and the gun rattled in his hands. Noreen approached and took the gun from him. He seemed relieved as Noreen slipped the weapon out of his hands.

"It's okay, Dennis," Noreen said. "I do respect you. But now you've messed up. And I need you to get on your knees."

This wasn't looking good for the last Turtle. I elbowed Miss May and nodded toward the door. We backed slowly toward the exit.

"You two aren't going anywhere." Noreen cut behind us and locked the door. "On your knees beside him."

"You don't want to do this," Miss May said.

"What are you even planning to do?" I asked. "Some kind of firing squad? You'll never get away with that."

"Shut up, cheesy Chelsea! I'm trying to think."

Dennis hung his head. "Don't make her angry. She's a beautiful woman. But she gets very angry." He lowered his voice. "We were lovers once, you know."

"Really?" I asked, with a note of incredulity in my voice.

Dennis nodded. "I used to be very handsome. Noreen liked my full head of hair."

"I said, 'shut up!'" Noreen pointed the gun at us with renewed fury.

"We better do what she says," Miss May said.

"Thank you," Noreen said. Then she turned to the windows and closed the blinds. I don't normally have quick reflexes, but for some reason, in that split second when Noreen's back was to me, I had the courage and presence of mind to act.

I swung my left foot out and around in a wide half-circle, and the full force of my kick hit right at Noreen's calves, sweeping her legs out from under her. *Reminder to self: Thank Master Skinner for your karate skills.* Noreen yelped as she fell. She dropped the gun and it spun across the floor toward Dennis. Miss May dove toward the gun, but she and Dennis reached it at the same time.

Noreen tackled me and clawed at my face. "No," I yelled. "Get off of me!" Noreen and I were both pretty bad at fighting, and we rolled and flopped around on the floor like a couple of overweight seals.

Miss May was not faring much better. Dennis was stronger than her, and he quickly wrestled the gun away.

"I have the gun again," he declared. "Now I'm the boss!"

Another voice boomed from behind the racks of clothes. "Not for long," the voice said. *I recognize that voice,* I thought, with a grateful sigh.

Sure enough, Wayne entered from the back, gun trained on Dennis. "Drop it, Turtle."

"Drats!" Dennis lowered the gun and got back on his knees. "I'm just the getaway driver!"

Wayne tossed me a pair of handcuffs. "You want to do the honors?"

I blanched. "Me? Is that legal?"

Wayne shrugged. The respect felt good. But I had no idea how to work handcuffs. I tossed them back.

"Maybe next time."

29

JAILBIRD, JAILBREAK

I entered the police department later that night with my head held high. I had helped catch not one, but two criminals. I had karated a woman and kept her from killing three people, including me. *That may not be a feeling with which many people are familiar but let me tell you... it's nice.* I held my head even higher when I saw that it was Wayne, rather than Hercules, at the front desk.

"Where's Hercules?" I asked.

Wayne looked up from his computer. "Oh hey. He's on assignment. Something about a Big Bertha pothole on Commerce Street?"

"I heard all about it," I said. "Sounds more like a regular hole to me."

"I agree," Wayne said. "Those measurements are astronomical for a pothole."

There was a brief silence, then Wayne and I both burst into nervous giggles. OK, I burst into nervous giggles and Wayne let out a single guffaw. *But he was nervous, I could tell.*

"OK," I said, bracing myself for what was to come. "Give me the speech."

"What speech?"

"The one where you say my aunt and I shouldn't be doing this. We're just ladies who bake cookies and pick apples. We don't know what we're doing, we could've been in real danger and Teeny is a wildcard liability. Etcetera, etcetera."

"I wasn't going to say any of that," Wayne said. "You and your aunt are decent detectives. Not real detectives with the twelve years of training I have, mind you. But I can't argue with results."

"Oh. Well. Thank you." I smirked. "Twelve years, huh? Shouldn't you be chief of police by now? What do you do on that computer all day, play solitaire?"

"More of a hearts man, actually," Wayne said.

I laughed. "By the way, how did you figure out Noreen was behind all this?"

"I didn't. But I've had a tail on Dennis since Linda's funeral."

"So that's how you ended up at the dry-cleaners the minute after he did."

Wayne nodded.

"I guess that means we were working the case from different angles. And we both turned out to be right."

"That's one way to look at it," Wayne said. "Another way is, I saved a couple of amateur sleuths from being gunned down at a local business. Thereby also saving a lot of nice clothes from being ruined by blood spatter."

"I thought you said we were decent detectives," I protested. "Besides! You did not save us. I saved us by karate-kicking Noreen's legs right out from under her. Have you not heard about my mad karate skills?"

"Oh, I've heard," Wayne said. "I'm going to have to check out Master Skinner's dojo for myself. He trained you well.

Seems he's quite the sensei."

"He is. If he managed to mold my uncoordinated limbs into blue belt shape, imagine what he could do with your um..." *Stunning physique? Masculine splendor? Ginormous muscles?* "Your uh...the body...the limbs you have."

Wayne laughed and stood up. "Wait here. I'll get KP."

Moments later, KP emerged from the holding area clutching a small plastic bag with his personal effects. He actually looked pretty good, like he'd gotten a little rest and all those potatoes were agreeing with him.

"Are you ready to go home, KP?" I asked. "Or do you want to stay another night?"

"There is something nice about that cell. But my flight to Hawaii leaves in under 36 hours. I gotta get packing."

I laughed. "I hope you're hungry. Miss May's throwing a party in the event barn in your honor. A sort of welcome home/sendoff combo. An aloha party, I guess." *Hello and farewell in one.*

"Oh, I can always eat." KP patted his stomach. "But I thought you did your mystery wrap parties at Grandma's? Isn't Teeny going to be offended?"

"She's swamped at the restaurant. Pete took over the kitchen. He's cooking up this fancy organic stuff that people are loving. Grandma's has been so crowded that Teeny barely even had time to throw a fit about missing the big arrest again!"

KP chuckled. "Good. I want to get back to the orchard anyway. Spend some quality time with that little horse of mine. Poor See-Saw. Probably dying of lonesomeness." KP looked from me, to Wayne, then back to me again. "I'll be in the car."

I watched KP leave then looked over at Wayne. "How about you? Hungry?"

Wayne smirked. "You want me to come to KP's party?"

"Just wondering if you're hungry."

"Maybe I'll stop by," he said. "I mean, if you're asking me out. It'd be rude to say no."

I gave Wayne a playful shove. "Whatever."

"Hey. You're assaulting an officer of the law. That's a federal offense."

I grinned. "So lock me up."

KP's aloha party was a smash hit. The bash was even more well-attended than the Candy Apple Hoedown. Maybe it was because people were happy that KP had finally been freed or — more likely — because Miss May gave a complimentary candy apple to everyone who showed up.

Whatever the reason, people showed up in droves, and KP's wrongful incarceration and subsequent release turned out to be great for business. Miss May booked dozens of apple-picking appointments and pre-sold lots of Christmas trees for the winter.

Plus, Liz's Gazette article about the unfortunate fates of the Manhattan Turtles had been picked up and reprinted in several regional newspapers, so we even had some first-time visitors to the orchard. And each one of them was eager to meet the famed local sleuths who had cracked the case open wider than the Commerce Street pothole.

Oddly, it seemed like the string of murders in Pine Grove might be turning our town into a popular destination in the area. People's curiosity brought them in, and Pine Grove's charm and hospitality made the newcomers stick around for a few days. Some even stayed the weekend at the Dragonfly

Inn. I had the feeling that our slow business was about to speed up.

After the last guest left, I convinced Miss May to get off her feet and go to bed, and I promised to clean up the barn by myself. So I was sweeping up alone when Wayne arrived.

"Party over?" Wayne asked.

I wasn't expecting to hear his coarse voice in the dark barn, so when he spoke, I shrieked and almost jumped straight out of my party outfit. Wayne laughed, but I played it off like I was totally calm.

"Been over for a while now," I said. "You must have just finished the world's longest game of hearts."

"Hercules needed help down by the pothole. Twisted his ankle and couldn't get up."

"That is the most pathetic thing I've ever heard."

Wayne laughed and strode toward me. "Can I help clean up?"

"I'm almost done here."

Wayne came right up to me and stopped when he was only inches away. He placed a hand on the broom handle. "Please. I insist. I missed the whole party."

Just then, a romantic ballad blasted from inside the farmhouse. I blushed and shook my head. "Miss May must be watching from inside."

Wayne turned and waved up at the farmhouse. The lights in the house switched off but the music stayed on.

He chuckled. "I think your aunt wants us to dance."

Wayne gently pried the broom from my hands and set it aside. He turned back and extended a hand to me.

I smiled and took his hand. He wrapped his arm around my waist. I leaned in toward him, stepping awkwardly at first and out of time with the music. It was a slow song, but time seemed to be in fast-forward, and I couldn't persuade my legs to move at the right speed. But Wayne guided me, keeping a steady rhythm and being chivalrous enough not to protest when I repeatedly stepped on his toes.

I looked down, closing my eyes and surrendering to the feeling of comfort I had in Wayne's arms. It was the first time I had relaxed since the moment I had met Linda Turtle. I let myself sink into Wayne's solid chest, relishing our first dance. *Nothing could ruin this moment.*

Then my phone rang.

I grumbled and checked the ID. *You guessed it. Mike.*

"You can take that," said Wayne. "If you need to."

"I think... Maybe I do."

I fumbled for the phone but dropped it. The plastic case clattered against the barn floor. *You cannot live a plastic life*, I thought. I looked back at Wayne.

"You want to keep dancing while we talk?"

"Your hand-eye is already pretty strained," Wayne said, but wrapped his arm around me as I answered the phone.

"Hello," I said. I could tell Mike wanted to talk, but I didn't give him much attention. "Yeah. I can't talk. No. As it happens, I'm slow-dancing with a handsome police officer." *Mike didn't love that.* "No. I don't want to talk about it. And I don't want to talk about what happened. I don't think it's a good idea. Not now. Not ever. Bye!"

Wayne raised his eyebrows after I hung up. "Who was that?" He asked.

"Telemarketer. I think he'll stop calling after tonight."

Wayne spun me under his arm, then I twirled back toward him. We kept dancing even after the end of the song. And I forgot all about the murders and everything else bad in the whole wide world.

Until I discovered the next body, that is. But that's a story for another day.

The End

Dear Reader,

Thank you for joining Chelsea, Teeny and Miss May on this autumn adventure. The girls had fun on that mystery, so I hope you did too.

The next story in this series is called *Berried Alive*.

You'll love this cozy because everyone loves mysteries with quirky detectives and a compelling bad guy.

Search *Berried Alive* on Amazon to grab your copy today.

Chelsea